"Know what this is?" Hank asked.

Claire shook her head. "No."

"Part of a label. From a bottle of rum," Hank said.

"Rum?" Claire gave him a skeptical look. "Where would Tink get rum? Whiskey, gin, grain alcohol, sure, but for rum you'd have to be—"

Hank was watching her with his usual cocky grin. He arched his eyebrows. "Have to be what?" he prompted.

She was silent.

"Claire, tell me, what do they serve at that speakeasy that you have so much fun at?" he asked.

"Not rum, I've never seen rum there," Claire insisted.

"Mmhmm." Hank scratched his ear. "And what they *do* serve, where do they get that? From the Ladies' Temperance League?"

Frowning, Claire turned away, the scrap of paper in her hand.

"Claire, you know perfectly well that speakeasies are run by bootleggers, and rum-running is as old as Massachusetts. Your precious little quiet town has its own share of desperadoes, and nothing you can say will change that. Tink was smuggling rum, and it looks like it got him murdered."

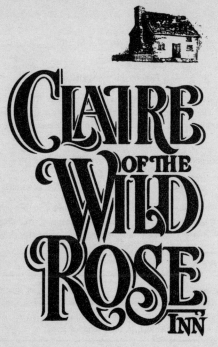

CLAIRE OF THE WILD ROSE INN

JENNIFER ARMSTRONG

BANTAM BOOKS

New York • Toronto • London • Sydney • Auckland

RL 5.0, age 012 and up

CLAIRE OF THE WILD ROSE INN

A Bantam Book/August 1994

The Starfire logo is a registered trademark of Bantam Books,
a division of Bantam Doubleday Dell Publishing Group, Inc.
Registered in U.S. Patent and Trademark Office and elsewhere.

ISBN 0-553-29911-5

Published simultaneously in the United States and Canada

---

*Bantam Books are published by Bantam Books, a division of Bantam Doubleday
Dell Publishing Group, Inc. Its trademark, consisting of the words "Bantam Books"
and the portrayal of a rooster, is Registered in U.S. Patent and Trademark Office
and in other countries. Marca Registrada. Bantam Books, 1540 Broadway, New
York, New York 10036.*

PRINTED IN THE UNITED STATES OF AMERICA

OPM   0 9 8 7 6 5 4 3 2 1

1928

Chapter One

A HANDFUL OF dry September leaves whispered along the gutter as Claire MacKenzie hurried through the alley. In front of an old tavern she stopped to survey the street. Marblehead was quiet, as it was every night. Prohibition had pulled the shades down nine years earlier and the town looked as sober as a minister. A single lighted window cast an oblong of yellow on the pavement.

Claire glanced behind her and then opened the front door of the Ship Inn. A stout young man perched on a stool looked over the top of the *Racing Form* at her. Behind the polished desk where he sat was a padded door, and to the right, a staircase led up to travelers' rooms.

"Inquiring about accommodations?" he asked out of the side of his mouth.

Claire shut the door carefully behind her. "Not exactly."

1

He looked her up and down and shifted his bulk on the stool. "Some other business, then."

"You could say that," Claire replied. She met his gaze without blinking.

"Name?"

"You know my name perfectly well, Zeke Penworthy. What do you think this is, a radio play?"

Zeke's face stretched in a grin. "Can't blame me for trying to make some drama, Claire. It's a boring job, sitting here all night."

"You aren't going to make me say some kind of password, are you?" Claire asked, her gray eyes twinkling.

He chuckled. "Nah. Say, I got my motorboat fixed, take it out anytime you want. The key's on a hook under the bow," he said with a smile. He'd been sweet on Claire for years.

"Hey, thanks, Zeke," Claire said, giving him a friendly pat on the arm. "I'd like to."

"Anytime, Claire." He gestured behind him. "Go on in."

Smiling now, Claire passed by him and put her shoulder to the padded door. The door resisted her, as though a flood were pressing against it from the inside, but at last the door swung back and a burst of light and jazz and voices and fast dancing poured over her. She stepped inside and shut the door on the speakeasy's bouncer.

For a moment she paused to adjust to the noise and brightness. Trumpets blared from the gramophone and a cloud of cigarette smoke filled the room. Wherever she looked, familiar Marbleheaders were dancing and talking and taking much-deserved—if illegal—refreshment. Claire squinted against the stinging smoke and tried to spot any of her friends among the dancers and the crowded tables.

"Claire!"

A girl seated at a table across the room waved to her through the smoky haze, and Claire raised her hand in return. The music was deafening.

"Hi, Kitty!" she called back.

Kitty Trelawney beckoned with a coffee cup, and Claire began to edge through the crowd, already itching to dance and have some fun after a long day's work. Before she had taken four steps, the music changed to a Charleston, and someone swooped down on her from the side and swept her into a whirlwind.

"Thought you'd never get here!" her partner shouted above the noise.

Claire spun backward and then forward again and looked up into her younger brother's smiling face. "I had work to do!" Claire shouted, swinging her arms and kicking back with her legs. She let out a scream of laughter. "Oh! My skirt's too narrow for the Charleston!"

"You should wear one of those flapper dresses," Bob teased her. His boyish face was flushed with dancing and laughter—and other stimulants. "Like those lookers over there!" he added.

Claire glanced over her shoulder. Two of the women dancing were dressed in the height of jazz fashion: they wore short, straight, heavily beaded shifts that glittered

3

and swished as they danced, and both women's hair was cut short and marcelled in tight, vampish curls on their foreheads. Their escorts were dressed in tuxedos, and one man wore his white hair slicked back like Valentino's. Claire had seen him there before several times.

"Pretty swelegant, huh?" Bob panted.

"I'll say," Claire agreed. "But you know I've only got one dress like that, and it's for special occasions."

"What could be more special than this?" Grinning, Bob caught her by the hand and spun her across to his other side with such force that she almost lost her balance. "Hang on!" he shouted.

Claire released her hand from Bob's and shook her head. "Oh, no you don't," she said, laughing. "You're getting too wild for me."

"You can't stop now!"

"I can do whatever I like!" she shot back.

Claire stepped away and ducked behind another pair of dancers. She was surrounded by faces—round, narrow, laughing, drunk, beautiful, and homely, all bobbing and swaying to the music as if the band in the gramophone had put a spell on them. Bob came after her, and Claire let out a shriek as her brother made a lunge in her direction. Laughing, she ran away.

"Whew," she gasped, throwing herself into a chair beside Kitty. She examined the hem of her wool skirt. "I think I ripped a few stitches in the kick pleat. If I hadn't been so impatient to get here I would've changed before I came over."

"That's what you get from dancing at speakeasies,"

Kitty replied, leaning her elbows on the table. "You fall into bad company and ruin your clothes. Those darn ol' wages of sin."

"If these are the wages of sin, I don't think I want a raise," Claire returned. "I hate mending and hemming, what a bore!"

"Does that mean you're going to give up dancing?" Kitty asked.

"Never!" Claire fluffed her dark, bobbed hair up from the back of her neck. "But jiminy crickets! Is it ever hot in here!"

Kitty smiled, her round and dimpled face as innocent as an angel's. "Some coffee might cool you off," she suggested.

"Coffee my foot," Claire said, drawing Kitty's cup near and sniffing it. It was legal "near" beer mixed with illegal grain alcohol to give it a kick. Claire knew she could get bootleg gin, too, if she wanted it. But she came to the speakeasy for company and dancing, not to drink. Even if she hadn't been reluctant to break the law, she didn't care for the taste of liquor.

"I'll get a Coke," she said. She pushed herself up from the table and edged her way through the crowd, wary of cigarettes being flourished in the air and careful to keep her toes away from dancing heels. At the bar, men stood shoulder to shoulder, making a barricade in front of the bartender, Zeke's brother, Larry. He was polishing glasses and arguing politics with a local house painter. Claire tried to catch Larry's eye past the wall of backs and shoulders, but no matter how she waved her hand, he didn't notice her behind all the drinkers.

"Hey, let me in here, fellas," Claire said, giving the nearest back a good-natured shove. "What does a girl have to do to get a drink around here?"

The man turned and gave her a gap-toothed grin. "Why, Claire MacKenzie," he said. "Make way, boys. We got a thirsty lady needs some service."

Claire smiled and nodded as they parted to let her at the bar, and she put one foot up on the brass rail. "Larry, I just want a Coke, I'm dry as dust," she begged as she fished a nickel out of her pocket.

"Sure thing, Claire." Without faltering in his political argument, the bartender reached into the ice chest, pulled out a bottle and yanked it up under the opener. Larry set the Coke on the bar in front of Claire and then went back to his polishing and politics.

"Sorry we can't be at the Wild Rose like the old days," a middle-aged man said to Claire with an embarrassed smile. "We would if—well, you know."

"I know, Mr. Carney," Claire said. She sipped her Coke. "You don't have to apologize. But we're doing fine just as a hotel and restaurant, you know."

"Back when your dad was alive, well, no joint could beat the Rose for good times," Mr. Carney said with a sad shake of his head. "That was the real McCoy."

"Handy thought he was smart to sell the Ship," another man nearby said. "Naturally, the police chief wouldn't think to run a speakeasy."

"And neither would the MacKenzies," Claire told him. "We run a nice respectable place."

The man raised his eyebrows. "Yes, but I thought Bob was planning to—"

He broke off as Carney elbowed him in the ribs.

Claire smiled away their embarrassment, concealing her annoyance. "Whatever Bob said is just a boy's talk. Selling liquor is illegal, or hadn't you heard?"

They laughed and went back to their drinks.

Gripping the cold bottle, Claire edged through the crowd to Kitty's table. Kitty was tapping her foot and lifting her shoulders in time with the music, and she followed with her eyes the two flappers who were dancing with their elegant dates.

"What do you suppose they're doing here?" Claire asked as she sat down with Kitty. She had to raise her voice above the music again and was getting hoarse. "We don't usually see their like once the summer's over."

"Suppose maybe they got drinking and lost track of the time?"

"Maybe," Claire agreed with a wry laugh. The music changed and Claire grabbed Kitty's arm. "I love this song!"

A lively Gershwin tune filled the smoky air, and Claire and Kitty joined in on the chorus. "He must be able to dance! He must make life a romance! I said a boooo-oy wanted, one who can smile, boooo-oy wanted, lovable style!" They put their heads together, hamming it up, and both girls became giddy with their own singing.

Laughing, Claire tipped her head back to sip her Coke, and felt someone behind her. She straightened in

7

her chair and turned around to find herself looking up into a pair of green eyes in a handsome face that she'd never seen before.

"Care to dance?" Green-eyes asked. He had a long dimple in his chin.

Claire surveyed him for a moment, and in the background a woman let out a raucous shriek as a quick fox-trot started on the gramophone. Green-eyes cocked his head to one side, and Claire suddenly felt she was being offered a dare.

"Sorry, but I never dance with strangers," she said, coolly appraising him.

"Then we should introduce ourselves," he replied. He scratched his ear as he smiled at her. "Hank Logan. Newspaper man."

Kitty put her hand on Claire's shoulder. "And she's Claire MacKenzie. Hotel manager. Now you're not strangers and you can dance."

"What if I want to finish my drink?" Claire asked, challenging him.

Hank Logan took Claire's Coke, tipped it up and swallowed the last half of the bottle. "You're finished," he said, wiping his mouth with the back of his hand.

Kitty let out a scandalized laugh. Claire was tempted to turn him down flat just to serve him right, but she liked the laughter in his green eyes. "Pretty confident, aren't you?"

"Bold as brass." He held his hand out for Claire's. "Well?"

"Go on, Claire," Kitty said.

"Since my drink is gone, it looks like I have no choice," Claire said, giving him her hand.

He pulled her up out of her chair and led her into the throng of dancers. She studied him as she followed, noting the way his brown hair curled behind his ears, and how the knot of his tie was shoved messily to one side. His sleeves were rolled up past the elbow, and his forearms looked tanned and strong. She thought he might be twenty-four or five, to her seventeen, but it was hard to be sure.

As he turned to her, the music changed to a slow tune. Hank grinned. "Hey, listen to that, Claire MacKenzie. The gods are on our side."

Claire let him draw her into his arms and she gave him a long look from under her lashes. "And here I thought the gods had just turned against me."

"Not on your life, Clair-de-lune. Mind if I call you that? It means moonlight," Hank said as he turned her around.

"And he speaks French, too, how enthralling," Claire drawled. "Are all newspaper men so cocky?"

"Comes with the job."

"Professional pest?" Claire asked.

Hank laughed. "Most girls don't think I'm a pest until our second date."

"Now we're on a date, I see."

Hank gave her a slow smile. "If you say so, Clair-de-lune."

"Oh, I wouldn't like to make statements quite as cat-

9

egorically as you do, Mr. Logan. After all, a girl needs some time to make up her mind."

Hank led her easily among the dancers. "You made your mind up five minutes ago."

"Then you know I'm dancing with you against my will," Claire said sweetly.

"And putting up quite a struggle, too," Hank replied.

Claire put her cheek against his shoulder to hide her smile from him. After all, he was already cocky enough for three men. She wished she didn't find him so attractive. It would help, too, if he wasn't such a wonderful dancer.

"How'd you get in here, anyway?" Claire asked him, looking up again. "And how did you know this quiet little hotel is really a speakeasy? The whole point is to be secret —there's no sign on the door."

"I was up from Boston for the day, visiting a friend in Salem," Hank told her, deftly turning her backward between two other couples. His green-eyed gaze was very steady. "He told me about a cute little gin mill in Marblehead where a guy can get a drink if he's thirsty."

His bold scrutiny was making Claire blush. She looked past his shoulder, and saw Bob, very flushed and unsteady, stumble into the bar and begin pounding on it for service. Her forehead puckered.

"And did you get your drink, Mr. Logan?" Claire asked in an absent voice.

"I take it you don't approve," he said.

"Oh, it's not for me to approve or disapprove what you do, Mr. Logan. I don't even know you."

Hank laughed. His hand on her waist was very

warm. "You're a cool customer. If the G-men come busting in, take pity on a poor guy and hide me."

"I promise on one condition," Claire told him.

"What's that?"

"That you let me say thank you for the dance," she said and stepped out of his embrace.

Hank raised his eyebrows. "What did I say?"

"You've said so much, it's hard to know where to start," Claire replied.

"Oooh, a sharp left hook," Hank said with a lopsided grin. "Thanks for the fight. I mean the dance."

"No, thank *you.*" Claire gave him a cool smile, and then walked back to Kitty.

"What a gorgeous man," Kitty gasped the moment Claire sat down. "Why did you stop dancing?"

Shaking her head, Claire picked up her Coke bottle and pressed the glass to her hot cheek. But the empty bottle had lost its chill, and she was just as flushed as ever. "I don't know."

Kitty chuckled. "I know why."

Claire met her friend's eyes and let out a breathless laugh. "Because he's rude and arrogant?"

"Noooo," Kitty drawled. "I don't think you stopped dancing because of that."

"Well, you're right, although he certainly is rude and arrogant," Claire said. "But I had to stop because my knees were so weak I thought I'd fall down."

"Most girls appreciate that kind of thing," Kitty pointed out. "But not Claire MacKenzie, oh no. God forbid she should let go for a moment."

Claire stuck out her tongue at Kitty, and was about to make a sharp reply when she spotted her brother again, and heard his laugh ring out wildly above the music. Her smile wilted.

"Speaking of letting go," she muttered.

Kitty followed her gaze. "Bob's pretty tight."

"Tight? He's practically spifflicated," Claire said.

"He was like that last night, too," Kitty added.

"I didn't know he was drinking so much," Claire said. She rubbed her thumbnail across her lower lip, frowning. "Maybe he's too young to be here."

"He's sixteen, only a year younger than you are."

"I know," Claire said uneasily. "But I thought he was coming for fun, not for serious drinking. He used to come once in a while to dance with me, but lately it seems he's just here drinking every night."

"Isn't he seeing Hope Carter anymore?" Kitty asked. "I thought they were such sweethearts."

Claire shook her head. "I don't know. She's all he ever used to talk about but suddenly he's all clammed up about her."

As she watched her brother across the crowded speakeasy, Bob straightened up and made his way toward her with the careful gait of someone trying too hard to walk the line. Claire was silent as he came to her table. He steadied himself against the back of an empty chair, opened his mouth to speak, and fell to his knees.

Chapter Two

"Bob!" Claire leapt to her feet and dragged him upright. Kitty stifled an embarrassed laugh.

"Sorry, I tripped," Bob tried to explain. The smell of alcohol surrounded him like a cloud.

Claire nodded. "Yeah, that big old chair just jumped right out at you. Funny how that happened."

"Most p'culiar thing," her brother agreed sheepishly. "Now, listen, Claire. I want to have a serious 'scussion with you."

Claire glanced at Kitty. Kitty rolled her eyes. "Here it comes again," Claire muttered.

"Claire, Claire," Bob said grandly. "We're missing the boat."

"Let's not start this again," Claire said, taking his hand. "Come on home. You've had enough."

"Not, no—" Bob swallowed and lowered himself into an empty chair. "Claire, we could open a speakeasy'd be so easy," he said.

Claire shook her head. "No."

"We'd be in the catbird seat," he insisted. "We're just speaking, uh—squeaking by at the Wild Rose. Can't make a go of it just as a hotel and restaurant, Claire. It was a tavern for two hun'red years. Hon'rable tradition. Like the good ol' days when we were kids. Parties, dancing—'member?"

"We're not going to break the law in our house, Bob," Claire said.

"Don't mind breakin' it here," Bob slurred.

The color spread across Claire's face. "That's different," she said in a firm, quiet voice. "The question is whether we are going to turn the Wild Rose into a speakeasy, and the answer is no. I don't care if the laws are stupid and unenforcable—"

"You can say that again!" Kitty broke in with a laugh. "Imagine Chief Handy trying to enforce anything. He doesn't even realize his old family home is a gin joint. He's too busy playing solitaire at the police station."

"And too busy pestering Mother," Claire added.

Bob was humming to himself, but he looked up at Claire with a crafty grin. "Tha's true. Been a widower a *whooole* year now. Must be thinking of getting remarried."

"He's not going to marry Mother," Claire said sharply.

"You're always so hard on the chief," Kitty said, leaning across the table. "And he's always been so nice to you."

Again, a flush washed across Claire's pale face. For

14

generations, the Handys and the MacKenzies had been rivals, and the Wild Rose and the Ship had contended against one another without cease. But it wasn't from old-fashioned family resentment that Claire disliked Chief Handy. Nor was it the fact that he was wooing their widowed mother, since Claire knew Mrs. MacKenzie had a right and a wish to remarry.

But Handy had rubbed Claire the wrong way since childhood. She knew he'd been sweet on her Aunt Laura Steele long ago but hadn't won her, and it made Claire uncomfortable that he was trying to marry into the Mac-Kenzie family again, especially so soon after his own wife's death. Claire could remember her father's memorial service ten years earlier: Handy had watched Laura and her husband with strange concentration and then left his own wife's side to comfort Claire's mother. He had been comforting Mrs. MacKenzie ever since.

"He's always telling her not to worry, not to get upset, he'll take care of things," Claire complained. "It gets on my nerves. She has nothing to worry about, business is just fine."

"If he becomes your stepfather you'll have to learn to get along with him," Kitty pointed out.

Frowning, Claire turned away from her friend. "Come on home, Bob, before you make an ass of yourself."

"Sorry, Sis," he said, sliding out of his chair and stepping away.

"Bob!"

Claire sat back and folded her arms, deciding it was

useless trying to fight him. Besides, she had come to the speakeasy to relax and have a good time. She glanced around, wondering what had become of Hank Logan. He had been maddening, but fun.

"Where's that wise guy from Boston?" she murmured. "I was sure he'd be back."

Kitty didn't answer. She was staring moodily into her coffee cup.

Claire leaned across the table, startled at the sudden change in her friend. "Are you all right?"

"Oh, um." Kitty drew a deep breath. "I'm fine."

Claire waited, sensing Kitty had more to say. At last, Kitty let out a weak laugh. "You haven't seen my pop, lately, have you? I thought he'd be here."

"Haven't *you* seen him?"

Claire's stomach sank as Kitty shook her head. Tink Trelawney was a notorious drunk. He usually managed to stay out of serious trouble, but he gave Kitty plenty to worry about, nonetheless.

Kitty toyed with the handle of her cup. "He hasn't been home since yesterday. He took his boat out, and . . ."

Claire reached over to pat Kitty's hand, not knowing what to say. No doubt Tink had gone on a serious drunk, but sooner or later, he'd turn up, repentant and broke. Poor Kitty would have to clean him up, only to go through the waiting and worrying all over again.

"Let's dance," Claire suggested. "That'll lighten your spirits."

Kitty laughed cynically. "Look around, Claire. The

preferred way to lighten the spirits is with spirits." With that, Kitty raised her spiked drink in a salute.

Claire sighed. She knew it was far too late to salvage any fun from the evening. "I should take Bob home. I'll have to sober him up a bit before Mother sees him."

"Your mother must know Bob drinks," Kitty said.

"She doesn't, and she's not going to find out, either," Claire insisted.

Kitty shrugged. "Who's the mother, you or Ellie?"

"Never you mind, wise guy," Claire said. She smiled and put her hand on Kitty's shoulder. "I'm sure Tink will turn up. He always does."

Claire looked around the crowded, noisy speakeasy again for Hank Logan and saw with regret that he was gone. *I guess it serves me right for cutting him,* she thought ruefully.

"If I see that fellow again, I'll tell him you've got a scoop for him," Kitty offered, reading her mind.

With a laugh, Claire collected her sweater and went off in search of Bob. She found him leaning by the door with his eyes shut. Claire put her arm around his waist.

"Here we go, big boy," she said, guiding him outside. "How are you feeling?"

He drew himself up as tall as he could. "Everything's jake, Sis."

"Sure it is, Buster," Claire said, gently combing his hair with her fingers. "Let's just take it a little easier from now on, okay? You don't have to go overboard."

"Sure, Claire, sure," Bob said.

"I would have liked staying and dancing a little

17

longer," she added. She tucked her arm through his and steered him down the street.

Bob gave her a sly look as they passed under a street-light. "Could dance at home all night 'f we had our own joint."

"Knock it off, Bob," Claire interrupted.

He sniffed. "If Dad were alive, he'd be all for it. Remember how much fun it used to be back before the war and Pro'bition? Dad loved running a bar."

Claire piloted him down an alley, where the fresh sea air hit their faces. A bell buoy rang mournfully from the harbor. Claire listened to the knell for a moment before answering.

"Well, Dad isn't alive," she said quietly. "That German U-boat didn't know how much we'd miss him, I guess."

Bob stumbled, and Claire steadied him. "I still think we should do it," Bob said stubbornly. "An' as man of the family I got a say-so, don' I?"

Claire was resolute, but kept her tone light. "We're not going to involve our family with gangsters and G-men."

Laughing, Bob dug his hands into his pockets, and his straight hair fell forward across his brow. "Gangsters, don't make me laugh. When did you ever see a gangster at the Ship?"

"You know what I'm talking about," Claire insisted.

"It's perfec'ly harmless, no Al Capones in Marblehead. Don't be such a minister, Claire. I don't need your sermons."

18

Stung, Claire quickened her pace. Bob muttered under his breath and ran a few steps to catch up. "Sorry, Sis. You're the swellest girl in town, you know that. The bee's knees, I swear."

"Never mind," Claire said with a wave of one hand.

They came out of the alley to the Little Harbor, and Bob began singing an off-color song. Lamps made pools of light around dry-docked boats, lobster traps, and fifty-gallon drums. Bob scooped a clamshell from the ground and pitched it against the side of a building. It bounced off with a sharp crack and disappeared into the shadows.

Claire slowed her pace and wandered to the water's edge, the stones and broken shells crunching under her feet. She squinted against the darkness to make out the shapes of boats at their moorings. While Bob threw more shells at the building, Claire squinted harder. One boat wasn't moored, but drifted. The dark form loomed against the water, moving slowly.

"Hey, Bob, there's a boat that's slipped its mooring," Claire said, crossing the boat yard. She walked along the dock to find Zeke's old whaling dinghy. Bob slouched down to join her as she felt under the bow for the key.

"I'm coming," he said, clambering over the gunwale.

"Fine, just don't fall in," Claire joked.

"Nice night for a boat ride, isn't it?"

Claire chuckled to herself. "We could motor out to Fort Sewall and attack from the sea. That'd liven things up around here."

"Marblehead would surrender in five minutes," Bob

said. "Let's commandeer that boat an' start the invasion. Full speed ahead."

Claire pulled the starter and the little outboard sputtered to life. In the faint light from the boat yard, the dinghy moved out across the water. Bob lay back against the gunwale and hummed. In town, a car backfired with a crack like a gunshot.

A whisper of apprehension blew across Claire's cheek with the breeze. "I know that boat," she said in a low voice. The bell buoy's tone grew louder as the wind shifted. "It's the *Kittiwake*."

"Tink's boat?" Bob snorted. "Mercy me, imagine my surprise. The old drunk."

As their boat came alongside the *Kittiwake*, Claire cut the engine and threw the bowline over a cleat on the larger craft. She made a quick knot and then hitched up her narrow wool skirt to climb aboard.

"Stay there," she cautioned her brother.

"Aye, aye, Captain," Bob said in the dark. "You can handle the whole 'vasion single-handed if you want. I'll be standing by. Make that sitting by," he said, giggling.

The two boats rose and fell with the swells, and Claire used the upward momentum of the next gentle wave to vault up onto the *Kittiwake*. She swung her legs over the gunwale and stepped onto the deck. The boat smelled of motor oil and fish guts and tar. Light from the boat yard dimly outlined the pilothouse. The open door was a black rectangle.

"Mr. Trelawney?" Claire called. "It's Claire MacKenzie."

There was no answer but the tolling of the harbor bell. Claire put her hands on either edge of the pilothouse doorway and leaned in. It was pitch-dark and smelled of cheap pipe tobacco. Claire desperately hoped he hadn't fallen overboard. It would be hard news for Kitty if Tink were lost at sea.

"Mr. Trelawney?"

As Claire stood in the doorway wondering what to do, the boat turned with the tide, and a stray beam of light seeped in around her and spread across the floor of the pilothouse. The slow motion of the boat drew the light into the corner, and it fell across a pair of legs in worn seaboots and dirty denim. Tink was lying slumped against the bulkhead.

Claire let out a sigh of relief. "Mr. Trelawney, there you are. Wake up. You're drifting."

The light traveled farther up his body, showing Tink's hands splayed on either side of him on the deck. Claire thought he should be snoring, but she heard nothing at all except her own heart suddenly drumming in her ears.

She swallowed hard and then picked her way across the pilothouse. She knelt beside Tink, leaning close to hear his breathing.

The boat shifted again, and the light spread up across his haggard face, his staring eyes—and the bullet hole in the center of his forehead.

"No!" The shock bolted through her, leaving her fingertips prickling. She turned her face away to fight nausea.

21

"Claire?"

Bob's shout came to her faintly, and Claire sat back on her heels, drawing a harsh breath. The air in the cabin was stuffy and cold. She gripped the tweed of her skirt, clutching it in her fists to feel the reassuring warmth and scratch of the wool. She began to shake.

"Claire, did you find 'im?"

"Don't come aboard!" she called.

"Did you find 'im?" Bob repeated.

Claire just nodded, again looking at Tink Trelawney's staring, dead eyes. Very slowly, she forced herself to touch his open palm. His skin was still warm. He'd been murdered very recently.

Claire stood up and backed out of the pilothouse into the fresh air. She leaned over the side of the boat and spoke to her brother.

"I'm going to take the *Kittiwake* to the harbor," she said in a steady voice.

"What's he done?" Bob asked with a chuckle. "Too drunk to stand up?"

"There's been—an accident," Claire said, tightening the knot that tied the dinghy to the *Kittiwake*.

"Always casualties in a war," Bob said in a sleepy voice from below. He yawned loudly.

Claire pushed away from the rail and made herself go back into the pilothouse. She was careful not to look toward the dark corner where Tink lay, but fumbled for the ignition key. She turned it, and the engine roared and grumbled into life.

Her hands shook as she engaged the propeller and

turned the wheel hard, and the boat lumbered heavily around in the water, towing the dinghy behind. Ahead, the lights of the town glimmered through the windscreen.

As soon as the main harbor swung into view, Claire tugged on the chain to blow the boat's horn. The blast was deafening in the still night. Again and again, Claire sounded the horn, until more and more lights began to wink on around the harbor, and headlights began to trail down through the streets. Floodlights came on one by one, and the docks and sheds and cranes of the harbor sprang out of the darkness. Claire saw people gathering at the wharf as she carefully guided the *Kittiwake* to a pier.

She cut the engine, and the silence was complete until the slap of waves against the hull and the approaching babble of voices reached her ears. As she stepped out of the pilothouse, she saw Chief Handy pushing through the crowd, tightening the gun belt around his waist.

"Well, looks like you've rescued old Tink," Handy called to Claire. "Did you need to call out the militia for that?"

Two fishermen made the *Kittiwake* fast and pulled in the dinghy, and Claire stepped down onto the dock to wait for the police chief. He strode toward her, his footsteps echoing off the water beneath the dock. Claire shook her head, unable to speak.

"Now, what's all the fuss, Claire?" he asked.

Claire tried to forget that he set her teeth on edge: it was no time for personal bias. She licked her lips, glancing at the crowd gathering just a few yards away.

"I found the *Kittiwake* adrift, Chief Handy. Mr. Trelawney is dead," she said quietly.

Handy's good-natured smile faded. "Ah, what a crying shame for Kitty. Heart, was it?" he said. "I knew Tink's ticker was on the bum."

"No." Claire had to clear her throat. Behind her, she heard the two fishermen go aboard. Any moment now, they'd burst out of the pilothouse with the news. Beyond Handy, Kitty Trelawney was pushing her way through the crowd.

"Kitty!" Claire tried to go to her friend, but Handy held her elbow. "Let me go."

"Whoa, hang on there. Not until you tell me what is going on here," Handy said.

Claire met Kitty's eyes helplessly. From the pilothouse on the *Kittiwake* came a shout.

"Tink's murdered!" yelled one of the fishermen, rushing out on deck. "Shot smack-dab between the eyes!"

Kitty's eyes widened and she began to scream.

Chapter Three

HALF AN HOUR later, Claire opened the back door of the Wild Rose Inn and helped Kitty in over the threshold. The kitchen was warm and golden, with lamplight spilling over the black-and-white checkerboard linoleum and the radio playing softly from the corner by the refrigerator. Mrs. MacKenzie looked up in surprise from where she sat at the table with a movie magazine.

"Oh, my goodness!" Ellie MacKenzie gasped. "What's happened to Kitty?"

Bob slipped in through the door behind the girls and leaned against the wall. He was thoroughly sobered up and excited by the night's events. "Tink's dead," he explained. "Murdered."

Claire shot him an angry look as she settled Kitty into a chair. The girl was trembling all over and too deep in shock to speak.

Mrs. MacKenzie put one hand to her mouth. "Oh, dear Lord," she whispered. "Poor child. Who did it?"

"No one knows. Is there any coffee?" Claire asked. She kneeled and stroked Kitty's hands the way she would soothe a frightened child. "Or better yet, brandy?"

"No, you know there's nothing like that," Ellie said uneasily. She patted Kitty's hair. "But there's coffee on." Ellie went to the stove, where the coffeepot was just boiling over. She reached for the handle and then jerked her hand back from the heat.

"Mother," Claire said patiently. "I'll get it. Why don't you put Kitty to bed? I'll bring up the coffee later."

Mrs. MacKenzie nodded, but then sent Claire a look of distress. "There's a gentleman in the dining room. He asked for coffee and a piece of pie."

Claire frowned. "It's a little late for dinner, isn't it?"

"I know, dear, but he was so nice, and I told him—"

"Never mind, I'll take care of it." Claire reached for a tray and began cutting the apple pie that sat on the table.

"He's a very pleasant man," Mrs. MacKenzie explained in a plaintive tone.

"Yes, all right, Mother," Claire said. She suppressed a sigh of impatience. It had been a long day and she had had a terrible shock. But it wouldn't do to let her mother's nervousness get under her skin. So she collected herself and then gave her mother a reassuring smile. "I'll take care of everything down here."

"Oh, Claire, you're so capable," Mrs. MacKenzie said with relief. She put her arm around Kitty and helped the girl to stand. "Come on, honey. Poor motherless thing."

"And fatherless," Bob added wryly.

Ignoring him, Claire picked up the tray with the pie and coffee and backed through the kitchen door into the warm hallway. Thirty years earlier, in her father's childhood, a fire had destroyed most of the Wild Rose Inn, leaving the oldest portion standing alone. The old tavern, built in the 1690s, formed the heart and soul of the new Wild Rose, which had been rebuilt around it in grand style. The prosperous young days of the century had seen the inn flourish, and in Claire's earliest memories the tavern had hummed and bustled with life and laughter, filled with townspeople every night. Her father, David MacKenzie, had been the perfect barman, with a kind word for all and a natural way with jokes and stories.

But then calamity struck the Wild Rose once again; Claire's father was killed in the Great War, and then Prohibition had cut the throat of the tavern business. Now a genteel but modest hotel and restaurant, the Wild Rose Inn heard only the faintest echoes of lively times in its creaking hallways. A dim memory of Tink Trelawney came to Claire: he had hoisted two pint-sized girls up onto the bar, raised his glass to them in a toast, and declared Claire and Kitty the prettiest barmaids in Marblehead. The other men at the bar had cheered in agreement, and David MacKenzie had winked at little Claire.

Claire cocked her head, as though listening to that far-off laughter. Tink's toasting days were over, and her father was long gone. But it did no good to dwell on the past, she told herself sternly. It was up to her to make the best of things, manage the inn, look after her brother, keep distress from her mother. Remembering her father wouldn't bring him back.

With a little sniff, Claire rested the tray against her hip, opened the door to the old taproom and stepped inside. The room was empty, except for one man at a table by the cold fireplace. His back was to her, and he hunched over a table strewn with papers. A cigarette smoked in an ashtray at his right hand. While she watched, he reached one hand up to scratch his ear and she recognized him in that gesture. It was Hank Logan.

Claire walked across the scarred plank floor to the hearth, and when Hank looked up, a wide smile lit his face. His tie was even more askew than before, and his hair looked as though he'd been raking his fingers through it.

"Decided to spend the night in town," he said in greeting. He tapped the ash off his cigarette. "I thought I'd test your hospitality again."

"How did you know where to find me?" Claire asked as she set the tray on a nearby table. She began to refill his coffee cup.

Hank leaned back in his chair and gave her his lop-sided grin. "Reporter, remember? I know how to find out what I want to know."

Claire tried to smile. But the coffeepot was rattling against the rim of his cup, and she saw that her hands were trembling. Coffee splashed onto the saucer.

"Whoa, steady." Hank laughed. "I didn't realize you'd be so shocked to find me here."

"It's not that." Claire turned away to hide the tears

that had suddenly come to her eyes. She made a play of activity with the pie and fork and napkin, rearranging them on the table among his papers and notes. As she moved a book aside, a tear fell onto the table.

In an instant Hank stood up and pulled out a chair and gently pushed her down into it. He reached over to the next table where clean place settings sat, and grabbed another cup. He glanced at her silently while he poured her some coffee and then set it down in front of her. He watched her for a moment and pushed the cup closer.

"Go on, it'll warm you up," he said.

"Thank you," she whispered.

"What's wrong? You look pretty distressed."

Claire shook her head. She was embarrassed to have let the shock of finding Tink's body get the better of her, to find herself so weak and so vulnerable to memories. She cupped her hands around the warm coffee, and let the steam rise into her down-turned face.

"Nothing, it's nothing," she said. She closed her eyes and saw Trelawney again and quickly looked up at Hank. She trembled slightly.

Hank noticed, but didn't comment. Instead he sipped his coffee. "I'm doing a bit of research," he announced, gesturing at the mess of papers with his cup. "A human interest piece on smuggling in the olden days. They say there's plenty of spots around this coast where colonists outsmarted the British navy before the Revolution. Seemed like a tie-in with all the bootlegging that goes on now."

"Yes, that would be interesting," Claire said quietly.

Hank shifted in his chair and stubbed out the cigarette. "See, what I think I'll do is find out if anyone in Marblehead knows about the history of those bad old days, do some local color, you know."

"Actually, I do know," Claire said. She pulled herself together and raised her eyes to him.

"Got a lead for me?" he asked. "Know someone with a checkered family history?"

"You're looking at her," Claire said with a watery laugh.

Hank whistled. "No kidding? Let's hear it."

"Well . . . This tavern has been in my family for almost two hundred and fifty years," Claire began. "One of my ancestors was quite the wily smuggler: John MacKenzie, bold, brave, and beautiful. He was famous around here. He and his partner—" Claire's throat closed up for a moment. For years, John MacKenzie's fellow smuggler was Nathaniel Trelawney, ancestor to Tink.

"His partner?" Hank prompted.

"Another local," Claire stammered. She didn't trust herself to speak the name Trelawney, just yet. She drew a deep breath and managed to smile across the table at Hank. He leaned on his elbows, propping his chin in his hands while he listened to her.

"My great-grandfather and great-aunts smuggled runaway slaves to safety before the Civil War," she added. "I guess we're a pretty nefarious family."

Hank waggled his eyebrows up and down. "Maybe I ought to stick around, then, and find out just how nefarious you can be."

"Oh, I'm as wicked as they come," Claire said.

"I doubt that, Clair-de-lune."

Claire had to look away from his bright green eyes. "Tell me about your work," she said. "Have you been a reporter long?"

"Oh, a while. I had a crime beat in Chicago, covering mobsters and murders, but it got a little hot for me," he replied with a casual shrug. "Actually, I'm taking some time off, looking for something to write a novel about."

Claire set her cup down. "A novel?" Her voice rose wistfully. "You're going to write a novel? How wonderful."

"Well . . ." Hank shrugged again, and Claire was surprised to see a bashful look on his face. He grinned, all brashness gone. "It's what I really want to do."

Claire smiled. "Some of my best memories are of reading novels with my father. I'd curl up in his lap and he'd read me *Treasure Island,* or *Gulliver's Travels.* Anything with a ship or a voyage in it, actually. We even read Captain Cook's *Travels.*"

"And do you still curl up in his lap to read with him?" Hank asked.

Claire shook her head quickly and looked down into her cup. "No," she said in a low voice. "He died in the war. In 1918. I was seven."

Hank tipped a cigarette from his pack and offered it to Claire. She shook her head, so he struck a match and lit it for himself, examining the red, glowing end through narrowed eyes.

"My father died in the war, too," he said at last. "He

was a correspondent for a paper in San Francisco and got shot up at the Somme."

"I'm sorry."

Hank shrugged, his eyes downcast.

"Is that where you grew up, San Francisco?" Claire asked softly.

"Mmm, for a while. Then I drifted around some, working for different papers, spent some time in Chicago and ended up in Boston."

"I guess you're a restless type."

Hank drew in on his cigarette and regarded Claire through the smoke. "I have to stop somewhere, sometime. But tell me about you, how do hotel managers while away the daylight hours?"

"There isn't much drama in it, I'm afraid," Claire replied with a smile. "During the summer it's busy with vacationers, but by this time of the year we're pretty quiet. Oh, of course there's the local mah-jongg club that meets here on Tuesdays."

"Do tell," Hank drawled. "How do you stand the stimulation of your job?"

Claire laughed. "It doesn't sound very demanding, but I've got plenty of work, trust me."

Neither of them spoke for a few moments. Outside, a solitary car rumbled past, and the house creaked in the way of old houses. The coal furnace clanked faintly in the cellar. Claire felt comfortable and peaceful sitting across the table from Hank with his messy ash-spotted papers and rumpled suit. He scratched his ear again, and they exchanged another silent, friendly smile.

Behind his brash manner he was really very kind, Claire thought, and she found herself hoping it would take him all fall and winter to get his research done, and the next moment she was looking at the dimple in his chin and wondering what it would be like to kiss him. She lifted her gaze to his knowing green eyes, and the color flooded to her cheeks.

"Will you be staying long?" she asked, looking down again and busily rearranging the silverware.

"Hard to say," Hank replied, not taking his eyes off her. "But I think so."

"Oh, good," Claire breathed. Then she cleared her throat and coughed. "We can use the business," she explained quickly.

He stood up, gathering his papers together and grinning at her as if he knew exactly what she'd been thinking. "And I can always use a good story, Miss MacKenzie."

Claire stood up, too, and gathered the dirty dishes. "I hope you'll be comfortable, Mr. Logan," she said in her most formal voice, focusing on her task. She couldn't meet his eyes without blushing.

"It's a really cozy spot, and I should know. I've been in a lot of places," he said, still grinning. "And maybe I'll see you at that speakeasy another time. We have to finish that dance."

"That would be very pleasant, Mr. Logan," Claire said. "Good night."

He chuckled and swung his jacket over his shoulder. "Good night."

Claire waited until the door shut behind him and

then sat down abruptly, the tray of coffee cups clattering on the table.

"Jiminy cricket." She pressed one hand to her cheek, and then quickly touched her hair, wondering how she looked. She let out a self-conscious laugh and picked up the tray again.

"Things are looking up in Marblehead," Claire said out loud. She smiled, and left the taproom.

Chapter Four

CLAIRE AWOKE BEFORE her alarm clock rang and dressed quickly, glancing out the window to gauge the weather. It was a fine, bright September morning, with clouds racing along the shoreline. Her room above the old tavern had one small window that kept watch over the harbor. She swung it wide, and a rush of cool, salty air came in. The milk truck puttered past the movie house and turned the corner of Front Street, and Claire watched as the milkman carried his rack of tinkling bottles to a neighbor's door. Then she picked up a cardigan sweater and let herself out of her room.

Claire tiptoed down the hall, careful not to wake their lodgers, and turned a corner to one of the new wings of the hotel. At room seventeen she tapped softly and opened the door a crack. Kitty was dressed, sitting on the edge of the bed, just looking out the window. The white morning light fell unkindly on her pale face.

"Hi," Claire said, letting herself in.

Kitty looked around. She wore the same dress she'd had on the night before, and it smelled of cigarette smoke and sweat. As Claire sat beside her and put her arm around Kitty's shoulder, the bedsprings squeaked in sympathy.

"How do you feel?" Claire asked.

"I've been better." Kitty held a crumpled handkerchief in one fist, and she began twisting it between her fingers.

"I'm sorry. I'm so sorry about your father," Claire said.

"Well, he wasn't much of a father, I have to admit that," Kitty said with a sniff. "Always drunk, always with an excuse. I worried all the time about him getting into trouble. But I never dreamed anyone would bother to murder him." Her voice quavered and she pressed one fist against her chin.

"Oh, Kitty." Claire tried to hug her friend, but Kitty broke away and crossed to the window. Claire sat where she was, knowing there was nothing that made a father's death hurt any less.

Kitty brushed the curtain aside with one finger and frowned out at the backyard. "At least you had the comfort of knowing that everyone loved your father, and that he would have been a success if he'd lived. But no one loved my father except me. The old drunk," she added brokenly.

Claire felt her throat tighten. "Your father was kind, and he loved you—"

"Well, anyway," Kitty said in a harsh, bright, tearless

voice. "Thanks for bringing me here last night. I wasn't in any shape to go home."

"And you're welcome to stay as long as you like," Claire insisted. "We have plenty of room."

"No, no thanks," Kitty said quickly, reaching for her purse. "I need to get home, see to Father's things."

"There's time for that later," Claire said.

"And I have to go to work, and there are arrangements to be made." Kitty was talking too fast, trying to gather her scattered belongings, checking her purse, picking up her wrinkled handkerchief.

Claire took Kitty's arms and stopped her. "Kitty, Kitty. The bakery will understand if you don't go in today."

"I have to go," Kitty said, meeting Claire's eyes miserably. Her face was puffy from crying. She tried to say something more, but gave up, pushing past Claire and hurrying out the door.

Claire stood where she was for a moment, shaking her head sadly, and then went downstairs to help with breakfast.

"Good morning," she said, joining her mother in the kitchen.

Ellie MacKenzie was busily frying bacon, and a pan of biscuits was fresh from the oven. The coffeepot gurgled noisily at the back of the range, and the radio played a jaunty dance tune. Claire's mother was always happy and confident in the mornings, and it was only as the busy, trying days wore on that the woes of widowhood made her blue. At the moment, she was humming and tapping her feet to the music.

"Good morning, pet," Mrs. MacKenzie said, offering her cheek to Claire. "Beautiful day."

"Yes, I suppose it is," Claire said as she kissed her mother. "Kitty left."

Ellie's face fell. "Oh, poor lamb. And without breakfast. We'll have to do something for that girl."

Claire smiled gratefully. "We'll think of something."

"It's hard for a young woman to be left alone," her mother said, shaking her head. "It's a hard world for women."

Claire watched her mother at the stove and felt a pang of sympathy. "At least we have each other and Bob."

"That's right, my love," Mrs. MacKenzie said with a quick smile. "I've got you."

Giving her mother another kiss, Claire grabbed the coffeepot and went into the tavern. One early riser, a salesman for a textbook publisher, sat yawning and rubbing his eyes, a napkin already tucked into his collar.

"Good morning, Mr. Felice," Claire said as she poured coffee for him. "You must be almost finished with your rounds."

"Two more days for Marblehead, Beverly, and Swampscott," he said. As he took a noisy slurp of coffee, a diamond twinkled in his pinky ring. "Then it's on to Salem."

"You must be the best salesman they've got," Claire teased him. "Are you sure you're selling schoolbooks and not bootleg whiskey out of the back of your jalopy?"

He set his cup down and stared at her. "Why, never!"

Claire laughed. "Just joking, Mr. Felice. What'll you have for breakfast?"

While Mr. Felice ordered, a few more men ambled in, and the outside door opened to admit a few locals. Chief Handy entered as Claire was pouring coffee for Zeke Penworthy.

"Morning, morning!" Handy called out to the room at large. He strode through the tavern, slapping backs and greeting each man like a long-lost brother. He sat at his usual table with a loud sigh of satisfaction. Every morning since he had sold the Ship a year earlier he had eaten breakfast at the Wild Rose, and showed no inclination to eat anywhere else. "Claire, pretty as a picture this morning!"

She made herself smile as she poured coffee for him. "Good morning, sir," she said politely. "How are you?"

"Fine, fine. How's your mother this morning?" he asked with a wink.

Claire felt herself stiffen. "She's fine, too," she replied. She turned away, remembering her tall, elegant father and his gracious manners, and wishing that she could stop being jealous on his behalf.

"I'll be back in a moment," she said.

She went out into the corridor and nearly bumped into her brother as he stepped out of the stairwell.

"Sorry," Claire muttered, swinging the hot coffeepot out of his way.

"What's eating you?" Bob asked. He sat down on the

bottom step to tie his shoelaces. His hands trembled slightly.

Claire shook her head, impatient with herself for disliking Handy. She hated to find herself being unfair. "It's nothing," she said in a tight voice.

Bob glanced up. "Don't start in on me, not when I've got a headache like this."

"I didn't say anything about you!" Claire replied. "I can't help it if you feel like a gutted fish this morning."

"Well I do, so don't yell," Bob pleaded.

Claire looked down at him. "Maybe it'd be a good idea to stay in tonight," she suggested gently. "We could play the piano together. We haven't done that in ages."

"No offense, Claire, but I've got other plans," her brother said, busy with his laces.

"Are you seeing Hope?" Claire asked.

Bob's hair fell across his eyes. "Well, uh . . ." He didn't look up at her.

"What's going on, Bob? Did she break it off with you?" Claire watched her brother, full of sympathy.

"Look, let's just drop it, Claire," Bob said, tying the last bow with a jerk. "I'm going to the Ship tonight. Period. The end."

Claire straightened the ashtray and magazines on a nearby table. "I wish I'd never taken you there," she said quietly. "Sometimes it seems like everyone gets so carried away over at the Ship."

"Maybe they'd just as soon go whole hog if they're breaking the law in the first place," Bob suggested. He winced and pushed his hair back from his eyes. "They can only hang you once, so you might as well have a good time while you're at it."

"If that's how Prohibition makes people behave, the sooner it's repealed the better," Claire said dryly.

"Amen to that, Sis." Bob pulled himself upright and gave Claire a sunny smile. "There we go, we're copacetic. I'm off for the newspaper—hope I don't find my obituary."

Claire shook her head and headed for the kitchen. Behind her, she heard Bob open the front door and mumble hello to someone coming in, and she glanced back to see Hank step inside. Her heart made a leap.

"Good morning," he called, shutting the door. "It's a bang-up day!"

Claire smiled. "You must have been out early."

"I like to stretch my legs before breakfast," Hank replied. His eyes were bright, and his hair was mussed by the ocean breeze. Claire thought he looked good enough to eat.

"Go on into the dining room," Claire said, turning away to hide her pleasure at seeing him. "I'll bring a fresh pot of coffee."

"Right."

The moment he went into the tavern, Claire flew down the hall to the kitchen and burst through the door.

"Two eggs over easy for Mr. Felice, scrambled for Zeke, is there any fresh coffee?"

"Just finished." Her mother looked Claire up and down while she put bread in the drawer of a large chrome toaster. "You look bright as a daisy all of a sudden."

"Do I?" Claire laughed breathlessly. She glanced at her reflection in a glass cabinet door. "It's a bang-up day, that's all."

"By the way," Mrs. MacKenzie asked casually, "did you have a pleasant chat with that Mr. Logan last night?"

"What do you mean?" Claire asked.

Her mother shrugged, and turned back to the griddle. "He's a very handsome young man, I thought, and very charming." She gave Claire a sidelong glance and grinned.

"Is he? I hadn't noticed," Claire replied. She opened the refrigerator, took out a bottle of milk and poured some carefully into a little cow-shaped jug. "He's bold as brass and thinks he's the handsomest fellow around. If that's charming, I guess he is."

"I guess so, too," Mrs. MacKenzie said lightly. Their eyes met, and both of them grinned. "Now go on, back to work. Shoo," Claire's mother said.

Snatching up the new pot of coffee, Claire hurried back the way she had come. At the door to the dining room, Claire paused to draw a deep breath and put a composed smile on her face. Then, ready for anything, she went in.

Hank had taken a table near Chief Handy, and as Claire crossed the tavern, he introduced himself to the policeman.

"You're Chief Handy, aren't you, sir?" Hank said.

Handy threw his shoulders back. "Guilty as charged, young man. Pleased to meet you. What brings you to our little town?"

"I hear there's been a murder," Hank said, sidestepping the question. "I was wondering what you knew about it."

Claire poured coffee for Hank and gave him a wry smile. He was after a story, no doubt about it.

"What makes you ask?" the chief said warily.

Hank looked up at Claire. "Just my natural born curiosity, I guess," he said with his easy confidence.

"He's a reporter, Chief," Claire said, more to bedevil Hank than to help the chief. "He's here to research a book about the old smuggling days before the Revolution."

"Looks like I landed in the hot seat, too," Hank said.

"Oh, I don't know about that." Chief Handy chuckled. "It might have been warm back then, but we're pretty cool and quiet these days. We're a law-abiding little town, not much excitement, and that's just the way we like it." He turned away then to talk to Zeke about Herbert Hoover and the upcoming presidential election.

Hank met Claire's eyes again with a skeptical look. "Doesn't he know there's a jumping speakeasy right here in town?" he asked in an undertone. "Can he really be that dense?"

She shrugged and moved away to pour more coffee for the other patrons. Hank scraped his chair back and waited until Chief Handy had finished his conversation. Then he raised one finger, as though he'd been struck by inspiration.

"Say, Chief," he said pleasantly. "Doesn't it seem to you like some enterprising types would take a look at this sleepy little town of yours and decide that what worked back then would work today?"

"I don't follow you, young man," Handy said. He blew across his coffee and took a sip.

"Smuggling. Rum-running," Hank said with a wide gesture. "Quick boats and daring souls thumbing their noses at foolish laws. Most folks think Prohibition is the most wrong-headed notion ever. Why not revive tried and true Marblehead traditions?"

Handy scratched his head, his once-red hair spiking up between his fingers. He squinted a bit as he looked at Hank's amused face.

"Well, well, well," he said at last. "I'm sorry to disappoint you, but those old tales are just fish stories. There never was much action around here, no matter what you hear. My family ran a tavern for years, and let me tell you, when folks get to story telling, a fish can grow pretty fast, if you take my meaning." He gave the men nearby a broad wink.

"Ever heard the line, where there's smoke there's fire?" Hank pressed, his green eyes glinting. He was clearly enjoying himself.

Handy chuckled again. "You're a persistent sort of guy."

"I usually get what I'm after," Hank said.

"Good for you," the chief went on. "But I don't think you'll find what you're looking for in Marblehead. You might want to move up shore a bit. Try Salem. There's a town with some history. Witches and all that."

"Oh, I don't know." Hank winked at Claire and

raised his coffee cup to her. "I like Marblehead, and I think there are some pretty bewitching people right here. I think I'll make some new friends."

Claire clucked her tongue. "Well, it's just a crying shame that everyone here has enough friends already, Mr. Logan, but we'll keep you in mind when we have some openings."

Hank choked on his coffee, and Zeke Penworthy let out a hoot of laughter. Claire gave Hank an innocent smile. "What can I bring you for breakfast?"

"Seeing as how I've got egg on my face already, I'll settle for some toast," he said.

Claire made a big show of writing "toast" on her notepad. "Got it. I'll be right back."

"She sure took the wind out of your sails, mister," one man said.

There was muffled laughter at Hank's expense as Claire left the room. Claire smiled to herself. Hank had offered her a challenge at the speakeasy when he had been so confident she would dance with him; she had accepted the challenge gladly, and now he had better watch his step. He's met his match in Claire MacKenzie, she thought happily.

"You look like the cat that swallowed the canary," her mother said as Claire returned to the kitchen. "Your father had just that same smile."

Claire grinned. "I remember. That's how he looked in your wedding picture. Like he'd just struck gold."

"Well it was a lovely wedding," Mrs. MacKenzie said in a modest voice.

"We should have more wedding parties here, Mother," Claire said eagerly. "We had them all the time when I was little. It would be good for business."

"They're a lot of work," her mother said.

"We could manage it, I'm sure," Claire pressed. "I'd be happy to do—"

"We'll see," Mrs. MacKenzie interrupted. She put her hand to Claire's cheek. "But I know I'd like to see *you* get married from this house."

Claire laughed. "One thing at a time, Mother. I haven't fallen in love, yet."

"You will, dear."

"Well, not until after lunch, at the earliest," Claire said, picking up a tray of orders with a grin. "I've got work to do this morning."

When breakfast was over, Claire poured herself a cup of coffee and sat with her mother and brother at the kitchen table. Ellie hummed along with the radio, and Bob propped his chin in one hand as he read the comics. Claire looked up from reading the international news and smiled contentedly as her gaze rested on their small family.

Then the kitchen door opened, and Chief Handy poked his head in. "Any coffee left?"

Claire's smile faded even as her mother's face lit up. "Why, of course there is, Jack. Come right on in." Mrs. MacKenzie went to the stove for the pot.

Bob scooted his chair to one side without looking up, while Chief Handy sat down beside him. The man accepted a cup of coffee from Claire's mother, and turned a bright-eyed look on Bob.

"So, how's the man of the house this morning?" he asked in a hearty voice. "Ready for school? Just because it's your last year doesn't mean you can let things slip."

Bob winced. "I won't, sir." The newspaper scrunched as he shifted his elbow so he could shade his eyes with one hand.

"He's a little tired after last night's excitement," Mrs. MacKenzie said. She put her hand to Bob's forehead. "Such a dreadful thing. Do you know yet who shot Tink?"

"Not yet, but don't you worry, Ellie. I'm on the trail," Handy said confidently.

Claire was tempted to point out that the trail wasn't circling around the MacKenzies' breakfast table, but she held her tongue and stirred her coffee. She doubted Handy could find a murderer when he couldn't even see that Bob was hung over, and it bothered her that Handy was taking his place at their table more and more for granted. He acted as though he lived there.

"Excuse me," she said, pushing her chair back. "I've got work to do."

"Of course, dear."

Mrs. MacKenzie hardly looked up as Claire went to the door. Handy began pontificating to Bob about the boy's future, and Claire looked back to see an expression of gratitude on her mother's face. Ellie MacKenzie had been the pampered daughter in a family of boys, and seemed to be perfectly happy turning over the difficult jobs to a man like Handy. Claire watched her mother for a moment, fearing the next wedding at the Wild Rose Inn might be Mrs. MacKenzie's. She left the kitchen with a frown.

All through the day, as Claire worked at the inn, she kept hoping to run into Hank. Each time she heard a footstep, she looked around in anticipation of renewing their sparring match, but each time was disappointed. He had left the tavern unnoticed after breakfast and hadn't returned since. Claire had been sorely tempted to snoop in his room when she was making the beds, but her mother had gotten there first. By late in the afternoon he still hadn't returned, and Claire was surprised to realize she was bored and restless in his absence. She wasn't sure she liked that realization. She took an apple from the fruit bowl in the kitchen and told herself to put him out of her mind.

Eating her apple, Claire went outside to the garden, which was full of golden September sunlight and cool blue shadows. Chrysanthemums and asters and lavender brightened the yard with their autumn colors, and the gnarled rosebush that sprawled along the fence hummed with the season's last bees. Claire fingered one lush red rose bloom, and the petals slipped through her fingers and lay on the ground like drops of blood. A sluggish bee hovered over the apple and settled on it. Claire raised the apple carefully to her mouth, and blew the bee away. When she lifted her eyes, she saw Hank walking toward her. She quickly unpursed her lips.

"I thought you were going to kiss that bee," Hank said as he joined her at the gate.

"I never kiss anything that might sting me," Claire replied.

"Smart girl."

He reached across the gate and put his hand around hers on the apple, drew it to his mouth, and took a bite. Claire gaped at him.

"You do help yourself, don't you?" she said, wide-eyed.

"That's how I get what I want," he said with his mouth full.

Claire tossed the apple into the gutter. "There, the bees can have the rest of it."

"Better them than me, right?" Hank asked. He grinned and opened the gate and strolled into the garden.

Claire stood watching him silently and wondered if he would offer to tell her where he had spent the day; she was all ready to tell him she hadn't the slightest curiosity about his activities. But he was maddeningly silent on that subject, and Claire refused to ask.

Hank broke off a sprig of lavender and sniffed it as he looked around. "This is a nice place," he said with a nod of approval.

"Oh, I'm so very glad you like our humble little village," Claire replied sarcastically. "Not that we can offer the same enticements of the metropolis."

He grinned. "What's this? A little on the defensive, aren't you?"

"Not at all," Claire said, bristling.

"I didn't mean to sound patronizing, if that's the problem," Hank said with an easy smile. "Sorry if I'm a little rough around the edges. The enticements of the metropolis—well, you know how it is. They tend to make a man worse than he ought to be."

Claire turned away. "Have you seen much of town today?" she asked, pinching off some spent blooms.

"Some, but I was hoping I might get a personally conducted tour," Hank said. "By someone who knows every inch of Marblehead, and every year of its past."

"Well, I might know someone who could do that for you," Claire told him, matter-of-factly.

"Can you do it right now?"

Claire laughed. "You think I was talking about myself?"

He nodded slowly.

"Well, since you made it so abundantly clear that you *always* get what you want," she began.

Hank threw up his hands. "Uncle! Don't you ever take off the gloves, Claire?"

She folded her arms. "Truce?"

"Truce," he said, holding out his hand.

She shook it. "For now, at least."

Hank laughed and held open the gate for her, and Claire went out ahead of him, ducking her head to hide her smile. A light breeze whispered along the back of her neck almost as if Hank had blown in her ear. She spun around quickly, but Hank was shutting the gate behind him. Claire laughed at her suspicious imagination.

"Ready?" she asked.

"Lead on."

As the shadows lengthened, Claire took Hank on a tramp through Marblehead, pointing out the oldest buildings, recounting the history of the town. At one house, she pointed out the third floor window from which a retired sea captain had made a sport of shooting gulls in the 1780s; in a garden around the corner a runaway slave had hanged himself for fear of being recaptured; in the park, the empty bandstand echoed with the cooing of pigeons, like the faintest notes of long-ago bands. Claire knew stories from generations of Marblehead history, and told Hank everything that came to mind with each familiar turning in town.

"You sound as though you knew everyone personally," Hank told her as they strolled through the harbor.

Claire leaned her forearms on the dock railing and gazed down into the dark, pungent water. The tide surged and sucked against the harbor wall and slapped against the tar-soaked pilings of the pier. She could see her own reflection down below, and Hank's beside hers. The sky above their heads was beginning to fade.

"It's my town," she said simply. "And I love it. I can't imagine living anywhere else."

She looked up. At the end of the wharf, the *Kittiwake* rocked up and down with the movement of the briny waves, empty and abandoned. A sting of anger made her frown. Murder had come to her town, and she couldn't help taking it personally.

Hank nodded toward the old boat. "They say you're

the one who found the body," he said. "Is that why you were so upset last night?"

Claire nodded, still watching the *Kittiwake* with a grave expression. "He was in the pilothouse. I thought he was sleeping, at first."

"I know. You can never quite believe they're not just catching forty winks," Hank said.

She glanced up at him. "You sound as though you've seen a million corpses."

"Not quite that many," he said, smiling wryly.

"I don't think I'd ever get used to it." Claire shuddered.

Hank pushed away from the railing and walked along the dock toward the *Kittiwake*. Reluctantly, Claire followed, and to her surprise, Hank pulled himself up onto the deck.

"I don't think we ought to snoop around," Claire said. "It's a crime scene."

He turned to look down at her and shrugged. "It's not sealed up. Come on. Snoop with me."

Claire frowned again, but followed him. She wouldn't reenter the pilothouse, however. Hugging her arms around herself against the chill, she strolled to the bow. The setting sun glinted off the windows on Marblehead Neck across the harbor, and the wind scudded along the choppy waves. Claire wondered what Hank was doing. She shivered.

"Not a single respectable clue," Hank called out cheerfully, emerging from the pilothouse. "I figured that bumbling police chief of yours would have missed a smoking gun, a written confession, and three desperate murderers hiding in the corner."

Claire let out a humorless laugh. "I don't think he's quite that incompetent."

"A guy can always hope," he replied. "How'd a flat tire like him ever get to be chief of police, anyway?"

"I don't know. The Handys have been around for ages, and they say the Ship was very profitable when Jack Handy was first running it, that it just about ran itself. Maybe he thought it was his civic duty."

"Give something back to the town that was so good to him?" Hank asked in a cynical tone.

"Something like that," Claire agreed quietly. "And besides, during the war, this town lost a lot of men."

Hank grinned. "The one man left standing gets to be chief of police, I guess." He stamped one foot on a hatch and looked a question at Claire.

"There's a cabin and galley below," Claire told him.

She joined Hank as he knelt down and slid the hatch back. The companionway led steeply down into the dim cabin. Without hesitation, Hank swung his long legs through the opening and let himself below. Claire paused for a moment. She wished that he were less nosy. Tink had been dead less than twenty-four hours—it seemed indecent to poke and pry so soon.

But then Claire caught a stray scent of Tink's pipe coming up from below and again she was shaken with anger over his murder. She scrambled down the companionway into the dimness.

"This place sure is homey," Hank said.

Light filtered in through smudged portholes, showing the messy bunk where Tink had slept off his drunks, a table scarred with cigarette burns and knife cuts, and a pitiful collection of tackle and foul-weather gear. There had been an attempt to brighten things up by adding a patchwork quilt to the bunk. Kitty's work, no doubt. But the place was even more dingy and pathetic for that one bright note, and Claire felt the gloom steal into her.

"What did Trelawney do with this old heap, anyway? Breed skunks?" Hank asked, nudging a toolbox with his foot.

"He had a few lobster traps, took summer people out fishing sometimes," Claire said. "Poor Kitty," she added under her breath.

Hank sat on the edge of the bunk, steadying himself as the boat rocked. "He can't have made much of a living at it."

Claire shook her head. "The Trelawneys have always been boat-rats. One of them was my ancestor's smuggling partner, the one I told you about. But the Trelawneys just never had any luck, except for Kitty's Aunt Maggie, who ran off with a rich New Yorker and was never heard from again. Usually they just manage to get by, and they usually manage to get into trouble in the process."

"Maybe he was bringing back a family tradition," Hank suggested from the shadows. When Claire didn't answer, he added, "Smuggling liquor?"

"He drank enough of it, but I doubt he smuggled it," Claire replied sadly. She went to a porthole and looked out at the water. "He was too fond of pouring it down his throat to make a business of it."

"Maybe so." Hank pushed aside the patchwork quilt with a sniff of distate. "Hey."

Claire turned. "What?"

He came to the porthole and stood beside her, holding something to the light. In his hands was a scrap of paper, a corner printed with the words "Puerto Rico." They both looked at it for a moment, and then Hank grinned.

"Know what this is?" he asked. His eyes looked almost black in the faint light.

Claire shook her head. "No."

"Part of a label. From a bottle of rum," he said, grinning even wider.

"Rum?" Claire gave him a skeptical look. "Where would Tink get rum? Whiskey, gin, grain alcohol, sure, but for rum you'd have to be—" She broke off.

Hank was watching her with his usual cocky grin. He arched his eyebrows. "Have to be what?" he prompted.

She was silent.

"Claire, tell me, what do they serve at that speakeasy that you have so much fun at?" he asked.

"Not rum; I've never seen rum there," Claire insisted.

"Mmhmm." Hank scratched his ear. "And what they do serve, where do they get that? From the Ladies' Temperance League?"

Frowning, Claire turned away and crossed the dirty cabin, the scrap of paper in her hand.

"Claire, you know perfectly well that speakeasies are

run by bootleggers, and rum-running is as old as Massachusetts. Your precious little quiet town has its own share of desperadoes, and nothing you can say will change that. Tink Trelawney was smuggling rum, and it looks like it got him murdered."

Chapter Five

CLAIRE TURNED ABRUPTLY and climbed up the companionway, pulling herself toward fresh air. The sky was layered with purple and orange and pink while the sun lingered on to savor the waning day. Claire leaned against the rail of the boat, looking down at the torn label in her hand. Something made her want to open her fingers and let it flutter overboard. If Tink had been involved with smuggling, then his murder was suddenly much more sinister. Perhaps some truths were better left hidden, and perhaps Kitty would be better off not knowing what had happened on board that boat, Claire thought.

As she stood there, she heard Hank's footsteps on the deck behind her.

"What's eating you?" Hank asked. "You already know he was murdered."

"I know," Claire said. She squared her shoulders, and carefully closed her hand around the label. Truth was truth, bitter or not. If strangers were muscling their way into peaceful Marblehead, she wanted it stopped.

"Don't you want to know what happened? I do," Hank said.

"You're right, Tink was murdered, and this is important evidence." She noticed Hank was grinning and gave him a puzzled look.

He scratched his ear. "I've always been a lucky dog, but this is too much. I come here looking for old smuggling lore, and land smack in a nest of bloodthirsty bootleggers. What a story!"

"Lucky for you, not so lucky for Tink," Claire said with deliberate coolness.

But Hank wouldn't be abashed. "Look, I know it's hard cheese for the guy," he said. "But I'm a reporter. This is what I do."

"Well it's not what I do," Claire said, hugging herself as she shivered. "Damn Prohibition," she muttered.

"Feel like a drink?" Hank asked with a startled laugh.

She frowned at him. "No. But if you're right about Tink, then it's because of Prohibition that he got himself shot."

"But without Prohibition we'd have no speakeasies, and you and I would never have met, Clair-de-lune."

Claire shook her head slowly. "I hate to wound your pride but I'd have gladly forgone that, if it meant Tink would still be alive."

He rubbed his jaw as though he'd been hit. "Hmm. I guess I deserved that."

"Yes, you did," Claire said.

"Can't blame a guy for being eager, though," Hank went on. "This could be a big scoop for me. Boston's crawling with reporters and bootleggers both, but in this sleepy little place . . . Who knows, with a little snooping, maybe we can crack the case ourselves."

"I don't know about that," Claire said, tucking the scrap of label into her pocket. "But we should take this to Chief Handy. I'm surprised he didn't find it himself."

"You are?" Hank asked, jumping down onto the dock and reaching up to give her a hand. "I'm not. He's as boneheaded a cop as I've ever seen."

"He is an old bore, isn't he?" Claire said with a little grin. "But even he ought to be able to do something with a piece of hard evidence. Let's go."

Together, they retraced their steps up from the harbor and went into the police station. Chief Handy was reading the newspaper with his feet up on the desk. Caruso was singing on the radio, but Handy switched off the set and got to his feet when Claire and Hank walked in.

"Well, what brings you two into my little kingdom?" he asked, hitching up his belt and beaming at Claire.

Claire glanced at the newspaper he had dropped on the desk. It was open to the advice pages, hardly urgent news.

"Aren't you investigating Tink's murder?" she asked in some surprise.

"Oh, I'm on top of that," Handy said easily. He folded his arms. "Now, what can I do you for?"

"We found this," Claire said, handing over the label.

"On the *Kittiwake*. It says Puerto Rico on it, and we're pretty sure it's from a bottle of rum."

"Found it on Tink's boat, eh?" the chief said. He gazed down at the scrap of paper, which was tiny on his broad palm. Handy rubbed his chin as he studied it and then walked back to his desk and sat down.

Hank leaned against the wooden partition and lit a cigarette, watching Handy with a wry expression. Claire waited impatiently for the police chief to speak.

"So?" she prompted. "I know we probably shouldn't have gone on board, but that's a solid lead."

At last Handy turned his attention away from the label and gave Claire a long, thoughtful look and then glanced over her shoulder at Hank. He chuckled suddenly.

"A regular pair of gumshoes, aren't you?" he said, closing his hand around the label.

"I guess being a reporter and being a detective are more or less the same thing," Hank observed.

"And Claire here is a real take-charge kind of girl, aren't you?" Handy asked. "You'll be the boss of us all, one of these days. I'll just have to watch my step."

Claire gritted her teeth. "I'm not trying to boss anyone."

"Hmm, maybe not," Handy said drily. "But it sort of looks that way from where I'm sitting."

"Maybe if you weren't sitting it wouldn't look that way," Hank said quietly.

The police chief gave Hank a startled look and then

laughed and stood up. "Got me there, son. You've got a way of putting your finger on things."

"You will follow up on this lead, won't you?" Claire asked.

"You can count on it," Handy said. He began ushering them toward the door. "And I want to thank you two for finding this and bringing it to me."

Frustrated, Claire stepped out onto the sidewalk and looked back at Handy. He stood framed in the doorway, his face in shadow. Claire had a sinking feeling that he wasn't up to the challenge of solving Tink's murder, and that poor Kitty would never know what had happened to her father.

"Thanks again," Handy said. "But how about leaving the detective work to the professionals from now on? This isn't a parlor game, you know."

"Sure thing, Chief," Hank said. He took Claire's arm and steered her away from the police station. "In your dreams," he added under his breath.

Claire looked up at him as they walked down the sidewalk. "What do you mean?" Claire asked.

Flicking away his cigarette, Hank nodded his head back at the police station, and the fading light threw the dimple in his chin into shadow. "A story drops out of the sky into my lap and I walk away like a nice little boy? If he thinks I'm going to roll over like a toy poodle he's all wet. You and me, Claire. We'll follow that lead on our own."

A rush of excitement brought the color to Claire's face. "Do you think we can? Maybe we could," she rushed on. "For Kitty's sake, I'd like to know what happened, and I don't have much confidence in Handy."

"I doubt he could find the barbershop if it weren't across the street from the station," Hank said.

Claire laughed and lengthened her stride to match his. Lights were winking on up and down the street, and a little girl's gleeful giggle sounded from an alley. A dog barked and a childish voice said, "Play dead, Sparky. Good boy."

The words sent a chill through Claire, and she felt a momentary hesitation. The word *murder* sounded in her head like a warning. *Murder.*

But then Hank looked back and smiled. Claire felt her pulse quicken and she ran to catch up with him, her thoughts rushing ahead.

"Imagine those bootleggers coming here to Marblehead," she said breathlessly. "It's such a quiet little town."

Hank laughed. "We met at a speakeasy, Claire, or have you forgotten that?"

"Well, no," Claire admitted.

"You like to kid yourself it's all in fun, just dancing and having a good time? That all those crimes you read about are happening somewhere else? Boston? Chicago?"

Claire stopped. The first evening stars were visible in the east even though the western sky was still painted bright. She hugged her arms around herself. She could so easily picture the interior of the Ship, hear the screams of laughter and the dance music, and see her brother spinning around and around and around.

"It's getting cool," she murmured.

Hank took her arms and turned her around to face him. "Listen, you have to face facts, here. If we're right, there's a good chance that whoever runs that gin mill is in on Tink's murder. And if Handy starts an honest to goodness investigation, that joint is going to be raided and shut down."

Frowning, Claire looked up into Hank's shadowed face. His hands were warm on her elbows, but a damp ocean breeze dragged its fingers across the back of her neck. She dropped her head.

"Closing down the Ship is something my family would have welcomed, years ago. The Handys always managed to keep ahead of us, somehow. But now, Jack Handy doesn't even own it anymore. I do think of it as a fairly harmless place," she said in a low voice. She pulled away from Hank and looked at the stars on the horizon.

"Sometimes I go there, and some of us get dancing, and I can forget about everything else," she added in a faraway voice.

"Forget what?" Hank asked.

Claire raised her shoulders and dropped them wearily. "Oh, forget what our place was like when I was little. When Father was alive, and before Prohibition. The Wild Rose was the most popular tavern in town, and there were toasts and rum toddies at Christmastime, and everyone was happy and nobody worried . . ." Her voice caught in her throat.

Hank took her hand and led her to a bench where they sat beneath a streetlight. He took off his jacket and draped it around her shoulders. A dirty newspaper scudded down the street, slid into the gutter and lay still. Twilight had brought melancholy with it, and Claire found herself yearning for brightness and sound.

"What are your worries, Claire?" Hank asked.

She let out a dry laugh and looked up at the darkening sky. "Oh, you name it, I'm worried about it. I worry when we don't have enough lodgers, I worry when the bills come, I worry when the summer season ends and the tourists go away."

"You sound as though you're the one running the whole show," Hank said.

"I am." Claire was tired and cold, and drew his jacket around herself with stiff hands. "My mother doesn't have much of a head for business, so I keep the accounts, and although I'm trying to put some money aside for Bob to go to college, it's—not easy."

"Bob doesn't look much like the college type to me," Hank said.

"Oh, he's sharp as a tack, take my word for it," Claire said. "And I want him to go. I want him to get out of here, see the world like my Aunt Laura did. He's stifled here."

Hank shook his head, the streetlight casting long shadows on his face. "That money would be better spent if you went. *You* should see the world."

"I'm stronger than Bob," Claire said. "I want to stay here in Marblehead and run the business. I'm happy here, but Bob is wild for some excitement. He used to have the most adorable sweetheart. Hope was a good influence on him, but now, well . . . who knows?"

Hank sat up. He brushed a stray curl of hair from Claire's cheek and straightened the jacket around her thin shoulders. "Claire, I've only been around for twenty-four hours, but I've learned something about you and your MacKenzie ancestors. You're fighters. You've come through hard times before and you'll do it again."

"You think so?" Claire asked with a hint of a smile.

"Pretty sure," he replied.

She met his eyes, and felt the tiredness leave her. "You must think I'm the biggest sap in the world, sitting here feeling sorry for myself."

"Not the biggest." Hank grinned.

"Well, I am going to face facts," Claire said, standing and squaring her shoulders. "Tink wasn't much of a man, but he didn't deserve what he got. If the Ship gets shut down, that's just too bad."

"So you're with me? No hesitations?" Hank asked, a genuine smile of delight on his face as he stood up.

Claire laughed. "I guess so, partner."

Hank threw his arms around her, lifted her up and swung her around. "What a team!"

"Hank! Put me down!" Claire gasped, laughing.

He set her back on the pavement, and they smiled at one another for a second. Then Claire realized that his arms were around her, and that he was still almost a stranger to her. She backed away, startled to find she was blushing, alarmed that he could get under her skin so easily. No one had ever made her feel so uncertain of herself before and she wasn't sure she liked it.

"I've got to get back to work," she stammered. "Mother will be wondering what happened to me."

Hank cleared his throat. "How about we meet later at the Ship, start asking some questions?"

"That would be fine," Claire said in a formal voice.

They stood awkwardly under the street lamp until Claire remembered she was still wearing his coat. "Thank you," she said, handing it back.

She turned to walk away, knowing that Hank watched her until she disappeared into the gathering darkness. As soon as she rounded the corner, Claire put one hand to her cheek and let out a breathless laugh. She almost felt guilty to be having so much fun tracking down a murderer.

Still smiling, she unlatched the garden gate. Claire heard a girl's tearful voice say, "No, I've made up my mind," and then two embracing figures in the shadows broke apart as the gate creaked open.

"Oh, it's Claire," came Bob's shaky voice.

"Yes, it's just me," Claire said. "Who's with you? Hope?"

Hope Carter, her long black hair streaming down her back, hurried past Claire toward the street. "Bye, Claire," she whispered in passing. Her running footsteps faded into silence.

Claire turned to Bob with a twinge of alarm. Hope had sounded so unhappy. "What is going on?"

"Nothing, it's nothing," Bob said angrily. "I can take care of it."

"Take care of what?" Claire asked. She couldn't see his face.

"I said I can take care of it!" he said, and brushing by her, stormed through the gate and disappeared into the dark.

Dinner was over and the dishes washed. Claire left her mother listening to a radio drama and reading *Life* magazine, and slipped out into the cool night. The scent of roses came to her as she went through the garden gate, as quietly as a breeze.

It was fellowship night at Claire's church, and she could see cars pulling up in front of the old meeting house when she turned the corner to leave Front Street. Cheerful voices came clearly to her. The church door opened and shut, spilling buckets of light down onto the steps. Women stopped on the doorsill, pulling off gloves, kissing cheeks, shaking hands with the minister. Claire stepped back into the shadow of a building, imagining their surprise if they knew she was on her way to a speakeasy— and to track down a murderer, no less.

"I'm not going to turn the other cheek," she whispered to give herself courage. She wasn't about to sit idly by while strangers came pushing their way into Marblehead and murdering its inhabitants. With that resolve clear, she made her way to the Ship.

Zeke Penworthy was on his usual perch behind the desk when she went in.

"Evening, Claire," he said pleasantly. "Go right on in."

"In a second," she replied, shutting the door behind her. She cocked her head at the *Racing Form* Zeke had left on the desk.

"Got a horse for tomorrow?" she asked.

Zeke lifted his round shoulders. "Looking for a tip?"

"Not the kind you're thinking of," Claire said. She lowered her voice. "I've been wondering. Who pays you?"

He screwed up one side of his face. "Come again?"

"You know," Claire said with a coaxing smile. "Who's the boss around here?"

"Well, it's a funny thing," Zeke said in a surprised voice. "I don't know myself. Larry collects my pay."

Claire blinked. "Your brother?"

"He don't own the joint," Zeke added hurriedly. "I only wish he did. Then maybe I'd get something better than this bum job."

"Hmmm." Claire frowned at the padded door.

"How come you ask?"

"I guess it's just a girl's curiosity. I have so much fun here, I wish I could say thanks to the owner," Claire said, and giggled.

Zeke smiled and waved one hand at her. "Go on in."

The moment Claire was out of his sight, the false smile left her face. She was ashamed of lying to Zeke, but she didn't know what choice she had. There was a murderer in Marblehead, and she had to be cautious.

Claire stepped into the bright, noisy speakeasy and shut the door. The scene was identical to the night before:

frenetic dancers, brassy horn music, smoke, and loud chatter.

But to Claire's eyes the light seemed harsher, the music coarser, the smiling mouths somehow menacing. Frowning, she surveyed the room and saw Hank leaning with one elbow on the bar, his tie loosened, a cigarette in one corner of his mouth. He was talking to the elegantly dressed man with white hair whom Claire remembered from other nights. As she watched, Hank turned and met her eyes across the room.

Immediately, he stubbed out his cigarette and took his leave of the white-haired man. He pushed toward Claire through the crowd, and she stood and waited for him. She couldn't help noticing how eager he was to get to her side.

"I thought you'd never get here." He had to lean very close to speak because of the music, and Claire noticed again how his hair curled behind his ears. She lowered her eyes quickly as he stood back, and felt the warmth rise to her face.

"How about a dance?" he asked loudly.

"I thought we were here to find some things out!" Claire replied.

"All work and no play makes Claire a dull girl!" Hank shouted and took her into his arms.

Claire let herself be swept away. She couldn't turn down such a good dancer. "Fine, even if it means you're getting your way again," she said. "How do you do it?"

"It's my charm," Hank said, his green eyes sparkling. "No one can resist me."

"Then how about using that irresistible charm on someone who can give us some answers?"

Hank turned her through the crowd, light on his feet and as suave as a movie star. "I thought I'd concentrate on charming you."

"It's useless to try," Claire said, and batted her eyelashes at him.

He just laughed and pulled her closer. "Sorry, Claire, but you can't blame me if I don't give up so easy. You charmed me without even lifting a finger, so I'm trying to make it square."

For a moment, Claire was at a complete loss for words. She put her cheek against his shoulder. She knew there was a ridiculous smile on her face, but she couldn't help it. It would never do to let him see how delighted she was, however. Claire knew he was handing her a line, but she enjoyed it all the same. As the music carried them around the room, Claire noticed the man with white hair again.

"Who is that man you were talking to at the bar?" she asked, glad to change the subject. "I've seen him here before."

"Says his name's Swenson," Hank said, glancing over at the man. Swenson was chatting with Larry Penworthy, who was polishing away at his endless collection of spotty glasses.

Claire frowned. "He looks rich. Why do you suppose he bothers to come here?"

"Maybe he likes the company," Hank said, smiling at her. "Maybe he likes talking to bartenders."

"That reminds me," Claire said. She stopped dancing and stepped out of Hank's arms.

"What did I say?"

Claire waved over her shoulder and headed for the bar. She gave Mr. Swenson a distant smile as Larry turned from him and said hello.

"Hi, Larry," Claire said. She glanced again at Mr. Swenson and then back at Larry. "Can I have a private word with you?"

"Sure, Claire." Larry walked down to the opposite end of the bar, and Claire followed him. "Now, what can I do you for?" he said with a smile.

"Got any rum?"

Larry's smile widened. "Rum? Quit fooling. Ask me something else."

Claire leaned her elbows on the bar. "All right, then. It looks to me like business is a lot better here than at the Wild Rose."

"Well, we've got certain attractions here, if you know what I mean," Larry said easily. "No offense to you and your ma."

"Think the owner could use some more help?" Claire asked, tipping her head to one side. "I'm an experienced waitress, after all."

Larry shrugged. "Well, I don't know . . . I could ask."

"Say, why don't you just let me ask?" Claire said smoothly. "Who's your boss?"

Larry's face fell, and he glanced back up the bar and out at the crowd. An overdressed red-haired girl from Salem tottered toward Mr. Swenson and asked him in a slurred voice for a light. The man took a gold lighter from his pocket and flicked it open, his eyes wandering around the room before he pushed past her and walked away. People milled around noisily, and someone Charlestoned into a chair and knocked it over. There were shrieks of hysterical laughter.

"How about you leave it to me, Claire," Larry said at last, polishing another glass with his towel.

Claire narrowed her eyes at Larry. She had seen where he had looked first. She cocked her thumb in Swenson's direction. "Is it him?" she asked softly.

Larry licked his lips. "What makes you think that?"

Instead of answering, Claire pointed her finger at Larry and pulled an imaginary trigger. In the garish light, Larry went pale. He set the glass down with a click and thrust his face toward her across the bar.

"Listen, Claire," he said, his eyebrows drawing together in a deep V. "Don't ask questions and you won't find out anything that could get you into trouble."

"You won't answer me?" Claire asked, masking her uneasiness at the stir she had caused.

"No, I won't," Larry said through gritted teeth. "Now go on, dance with your fella and leave me be. Stop asking dumb questions if you know what's good for you."

He stalked away from her, leaving Claire alone at the end of the bar. She drew a slightly shaky breath and then turned around to search out Hank. She scanned the crowd and spotted Kitty alone in a corner, sitting with her chin in her hand and a glass of liquor at her elbow. Claire meant to go see how her friend was and ask how the arrangements for Tink's funeral were coming along, but a sudden crash made her turn her head.

Bob was on the floor beside an overturned table, giggling helplessly. One of his drinking friends hauled him to his feet. Feeling sick, Claire made her way through the crowded room toward her brother.

"I'll take him," she said roughly, stepping between Bob and his pal.

"Suit y'rself," the man said.

Claire swung Bob's arm around her shoulder. He leaned against her and looked vacantly into her face. He was trying hard to focus on her.

"Claire!" he shouted with happy surprise. "My sis. Good ol' Sis."

"Let's get out of here," Claire said in a low voice.

"But's early," Bob complained. "C'mon, les dance, my fav'rite dance partner."

Claire's heart tightened inside her, and she blinked away a quick tear. "We can dance outside, how does that sound, Bobby? In the fresh air? It's so hot in here, I'm just dying to go outside."

"Awwww." Bob patted her shoulder and shook his head, but didn't protest.

Claire hustled Bob out of the Ship, struggling hard to keep him upright.

"Oh, Bob," she whispered, trying to steer him down the street. He became more of a dead weight with every step, and Claire had to prop him against a building so she could catch her breath.

"Bob, this is too much," she said, leaning against the wall beside him and closing her eyes. "It's too much. Lay off the whiskey, please?"

"Awww," Bob said again in a sleepy voice. "Wasn't whiskey, Sis."

"The gin, then," she said with a sigh.

Bob giggled and began to sink to the ground. "Wasn't gin either," he said, and put one finger to his lips.

Claire looked down at him with a sudden frown. His breath reeked of something she couldn't quite identify. "Was it rum?"

He didn't answer, and Claire shook her head from side to side. She was almost too tired to drag him home. She rested there, and Bob put his head against her knee and yawned.

"Is it something to do with Hope? Are you carrying on this way because she wants to break it off with you?" Claire asked gently.

Bob didn't answer.

"Oh, Bob. What am I going to do with you?" Claire whispered to herself.

Up the street, footsteps echoed hollowly off of buildings, and as Claire watched, two men paused near a street lamp. The light fell on white hair, and Claire recognized the dapper Mr. Swenson. Then, in the flare of a lighter, Hank's face leaned close to the flame with a cigarette.

Claire let out a sigh of relief to know he was so near. "Stay there, Bob, I'll be right back," she said, turning to her brother.

74

"Wait." Bob grabbed her leg and began to sniffle. "Don't leave me. I don't feel so good."

"I'll be right back," Claire said with mounting impatience. She pried Bob's hand off her leg, and turned to call Hank.

But both he and Mr. Swenson had disappeared into the darkness.

Chapter Six

"Mother, how could you let me oversleep?"
Claire asked when she hurried into the kitchen
the next morning, still fingering her buttons into
place.

"Oh, you seemed so tired," Mrs. MacKenzie said. She
patted Claire's cheek and went back to the stove, where
pancakes were ready to flip. "Bob, too," she added.

"It was a late night," Claire said. She reached for her
apron and tied it on, remembering how she had poured
Bob into bed.

"I know kids these days insist on making their own
rules, but I think Bob should be in earlier on a school
night," Mrs. MacKenzie added. "I think he's coming down
with something. This makes two mornings in a row that
he felt sick. What he finds to do with his friends until all
hours is beyond me."

Claire paused at the door and looked back at her
mother. Ellie MacKenzie was humming under her breath

as she coaxed breakfast along, but her once beautiful face was lined with worries. Either she really did not realize what Bob was up to, or she was wilfully refusing to see it.

"Mother?" Claire began.

"Yes, dear?" Mrs. MacKenzie looked around.

Claire swallowed hard. "Mother, I think you should know, Bob . . . he, well . . ."

"Yes?" The clock on the shelf ticked in the silence.

"Bob isn't doing that well in school," Claire said lamely.

"I know that, that's why I'm so concerned about him," her mother said in a tart voice. "Lately he's just a different person. He used to be such an easy boy."

"Yes," Claire said as a vivid memory of playing pirates with her brother flashed through her mind. He had always let her be the captain and let her wear the eye patch. And he would cheerfully fall down dead whenever she told him to, lying perfectly still until he spoiled the effect by laughing. For a moment, Claire could hardly breathe, so sharp was the memory.

"I think he's worried about Hope," Claire said. "I think she's broken up with him, but he won't say so. He won't talk to me."

Her mother sighed. "Poor boy. He needs a man to confide in," she said as she flipped a pancake. "Someone he can look up to, someone who can show him what it means to be a man. He's growing up so fast, and goodness knows he doesn't listen to me anymore."

"Or me," Claire said, more to herself than to her mother.

"If your father were still alive, he'd know what to do. It's just that Bob is so wild for excitement, like any boy." Her mother whisked the pancake batter, frowning anxiously. "Bob needs someone to look up to. Like Jack Handy."

Claire grimaced. "I'm not sure he looks up to Chief Handy, Mother."

"Oh, but he does," Mrs. MacKenzie said.

"But Handy's here all the time and Bob's still staying out until all hours," Claire pointed out.

Her mother frowned obstinately. "I'll ask Jack to have a talk with Bob, man to man. Then everything will be fine."

"I still think—"

"I know you don't have very much regard for Jack," her mother broke in. "But he's a good, decent man who's worked hard all his life, and his wife was such a trial to him. She practically drove him to bankruptcy but he never complained, not once. That's just the kind of man he is."

It was useless to argue, Claire knew. Stifling a sigh, she pushed open the swinging door.

"Oh, by the way, I almost forgot to tell you," Mrs. MacKenzie called after her. "Kitty called last night. The funeral's this morning at eleven."

"Poor Kitty," Claire said softly.

"I think I ought to go, don't you?" Mrs. MacKenzie asked. "It's not as though Tink was exactly respectable, but I do feel someone from the family should be there."

"I'll go, Mother. You stay here, I know funerals upset you. Is Mr. Logan up?"

"Oh, he left ages ago," Mrs. MacKenzie said.

Claire counted to ten in her head and then spoke in a steady voice. "Left for good?"

"Oh, no, he didn't settle his bill," Mrs. MacKenzie said, and then her face fell. "Oh, you don't think he skipped on us, do you?"

"No, Mother, don't worry," Claire said. "I only wondered—did he mention where he was going?"

"No, he didn't," Mrs. MacKenzie said anxiously. "Maybe I should go check his room, see if he did skip."

Claire crossed the kitchen and led her mother gently back to the stove. "If you did that, who'd make sure these pancakes come out perfect? You know I'm a hopeless cook. Now don't worry about Hank—Mr. Logan. He's not the type to skip, believe me."

But he was obviously the type to leave for the day without leaving word, and Claire couldn't help feeling hurt. For all his flirtatious talk and his claim that they were partners, he thought nothing of keeping her in the dark. His familiar manner was probably an old habit, Claire told herself, and she knew she'd have been wise to take everything he said with a grain of salt. He was after a story and that clearly came first, no matter what he said about being partners.

So Claire went through her morning chores with steady determination to forget him and stopped herself each time she was tempted to check to see if his things were still in his room. She refused to let his disappearance irritate her or wound her feelings.

"If he wants to play detective by himself, let him," Claire told herself as she headed for her room.

Her mother called to her from down the hallway as Claire reached the top of the stairs. "Darling, can you take these clean towels to number eight?"

Claire paused, regarding her mother from the whole length of the corridor. Sunlight slanted through a window, lighting the dust motes that floated there. Number eight was Hank's room. If her mother asked her to go . . .

"Claire?"

"Yes, of course," Claire said, striding forward and taking the linens from her mother.

She walked resolutely toward Hank's room, fishing for her pass key and telling herself that she was only doing her job. Her hand was steady as she unlocked the door and stepped inside.

For a moment, Claire stood with her back to the door, hugging the towels to her chest. She looked around, feeling as guilty as a child snitching pennies and just as eager to get away with it. On the dresser was a stack of papers, and a book lay facedown on the bedside table. Claire walked slowly toward it, tilting her head to read the spine without picking up the book. It was *Tess of the D'Urbervilles,* which Claire knew was the story of a woman ruined by love.

"Romantic novels, Logan?" she murmured, smiling wryly to herself.

Somehow, that glimpse into Hank's personality gave her some satisfaction. Still smiling, she went to the closet to put the towels on the top shelf. But as she placed them there, she felt cold glass skid away from her hand. On tiptoe, she reached up to feel at the back of the shelf. Her hand closed around a bottle. She took it down, suddenly dreading what it would be.

Claire stared at the bottle of Puerto Rican rum in her hand. Sunlight glinted through the pale gold liquor and made a dancing star on the carpet, and Claire's heart began to pound hard behind her ribs. Without thinking, she shoved it back on the shelf out of sight and shut the closet door.

Then she hurriedly left Hank's room and ran down the corridor to her own bedroom to dress for Tink Trelawney's funeral.

There had to be an explanation, she was sure there must be. All she needed to do was ask him and then she'd know. There must be a reason for Hank Logan to be hiding a bottle of Puerto Rican rum in his closet. Perhaps he had found it somewhere last night and was gone today because of some new lead that it represented. She dressed rapidly, her thoughts running from one direction to another. With shaking hands, she jammed a black felt hat down on her head and went downstairs.

"I'm going, Mother," she said as she stepped down into the foyer.

Mrs. MacKenzie was at the reception desk trying to sort through some bills.

"I'm sure I didn't order that," Mrs. MacKenzie murmured. She looked up as Claire entered. "Honey, can you make sense of these accounts when you get back?"

Claire sat on the edge of a faded velveteen club chair. "Yes, I'll straighten it out," she said absently. She fingered the doily on the arm of the chair, and then stroked it smooth. "I—I don't suppose Mr. Logan said when—"

The telephone cut her off, and her mother stood up to take the receiver off its hook before Claire could move.

"Marblehead four-four-one," Mrs. MacKenzie said. "Oh, hello, Jack."

Claire left the Wild Rose. She wanted to stop thinking about Hank. She wanted to forget the way she felt whenever he gave her his crooked smile or tugged on his ear. She wanted to forget she had found the rum. A furious scowl darkened her face as she strode down the sidewalk toward church. She had to think of other things, of Tink's murder.

She stared up at the sky and then looked around her at the town. Claire's neighbors came and went on their errands, and cars trundled sedately along the streets. A few cars had stopped at the church. Only a few. Most people had given Tink a wide berth in life, and it was even wider in death. Claire squared her shoulders and went to pay her respects.

The late-morning light fell in pale bars through the windows of the sanctuary. No more than a dozen mourners, mostly old men, sat in the pews. In the front pew, Kitty sat with a bowed head. Old Mrs. Lacey stumbled through a prelude on the organ, and someone coughed long and hard. At the front, by the plain Congregational lectern, Tink's cheap coffin stood on trestles. There was one small bouquet of flowers. Claire hesitated in the doorway, telling herself to go in.

She forced herself to walk down the aisle, past the solitary mourners. She felt eyes follow her as she made her way to the front and slid into the pew beside Kitty.

"How are you?" Claire whispered, taking her friend's hand.

Kitty didn't answer, but raised dull eyes to Claire's face. She looked older, somehow, since her father's death, and her mute grief made Claire's throat ache.

"Has Chief Handy found anything at all, yet?" Claire asked. "Has he told you anything?"

"No," Kitty whispered. "Not a damn thing."

"I'll find out who did it," Claire promised.

Kitty looked surprised. "You?"

Claire nodded. "I swear I will."

Kitty gripped Claire's hand, and they both looked forward as the Reverend Mr. Lacey stepped up to the lectern. He bent a compassionate gaze on Kitty over the tops of his glasses and cleared his throat to speak.

"The voice of thy brother's blood crieth unto me from the ground," he quoted. *"And now art thou cursed from the earth, which hath opened her mouth to receive thy brother's blood from thy hand."*

Kitty covered her eyes as the grim words fell on them, and someone shuffled his feet uncomfortably.

Claire's hand ached from her friend's grasp but she did not pull away. The minister's voice went on, and Claire stood and sat automatically for hymns, and mumbled the Lord's Prayer and the Twenty-third Psalm with the others. The service was plain and short, over in a few minutes. Six grizzled old seamen acted as pallbearers and shuffled out with poor Tink's coffin.

"Don't go with me to Burial Hill," Kitty whispered.

"Why? Kitty, I don't want to leave you."

Kitty shook her head. "Please. Please. I want to be alone—with my dad."

Claire watched her friend trail behind the coffin out of the church, and as the small cortege disappeared, a fresh rush of anger over Tink's murder made Claire clench her fists at her sides. She walked out onto the church steps, frowning in furious concentration. More than ever, she wanted to know who had killed that pitiful old drunkard.

Trelawney must have been in cahoots with someone, she was convinced of that. He had never been a leader and hadn't enough gumption to run any kind of smuggling operation on his own.

So he had followed someone else's lead. And that someone might well have been the one who murdered him. Claire walked slowly down the steps to the sidewalk, pursuing her train of thought as she scuffed through drifts of fallen leaves.

What sort of leader would Tink have followed, she mused. In life, Trelawney had been suspicious and argumentative, mistrusting even the most innocent "hello." It was safe to assume that he would never take orders from an outsider. So there was only one conclusion: whoever led Tink Trelawney into smuggling must be local, a Marbleheader, not some hard-boiled gangster from out of town. Claire felt sick at heart as she admitted it to herself.

Up in the belfry, the bell began to toll. Claire looked miserably around her. Ledue's Department Store was advertising electric toasters and pressure cookers in its windows; the barber pole turned around and around, the red and blue stripes spiraling endlessly; Mr. Bauman, the postmaster, whistled along the street, keeping an eye out for Mrs. Pool's fox terrier. The town was quiet after the summer rush and bustle and hurry. It was peaceful and prim, and readying for winter, neighbors nodding briskly to one another as though to say: time to get out your woollens!

And someone in it had shot Tink Trelawney.

Suddenly, Claire felt that she could not bear to stand in the midst of the town she knew so well. She could not bear to look around her and wonder which of her neighbors was a murdering rumrunner.

Claire hurried back to the Wild Rose and hauled her bicycle from the shed and then pedaled as fast as she could out of town. Overhead, a flight of geese made a V toward the south, their honking faint on the crisp autumn air. Claire let the bicycle coast down the slope to the shore, where the road struck out across the sandy spit that connected Marblehead Neck to the mainland. The wind whispered in her ears as she rode, and the noon sun struck hard and brilliant off the Atlantic. She let the bicycle roll to a stop and then hopped off, letting it fall on the sand. Claire dug her hands into the pockets of her black coat and trudged along the shore, hoping that the wind would clear her head.

Only a month ago, the beach where she walked had been covered with tourists, and the waters had been dotted with yachts and sailboats. The rocks had echoed with laughter and the gleeful screams of children, music had drifted down from the grand houses perched up on the Neck, and touring cars had been parked as thick as barnacles along the roadside. But now the place belonged to the wind and the birds and to the waves that curled endlessly onto the hard gray sand.

As the shoreline became rockier, Claire hopped from boulder to boulder with the surf crashing and foaming at her side. The water sucked at the weeds clinging to the rocks, and gulls wheeled screaming overhead. The sharp salt air brought the color to Claire's cheeks as she rambled along and tried not to think about the murder, or about Bob—or about Hank.

Claire shielded her eyes with one hand as she looked up at a storm-shuttered vacation home above her. The large houses out there sat well back from the water, with lawns spreading down to fanciful beach bungalows. Most were boarded up for the season, but in Claire's imagination women in white linen dresses were playing croquet there, while men in seersucker jackets smoked cigars and talked railroads and money; jazz played on the radio, and servants came across the lawn with trays of cocktails balanced on spread fingers. The rich came to Marblehead for fun, splashed their money and their liquor around, and then left.

But Claire was still there, and still needed to know how Trelawney had died. She stood on a boulder staring at the foaming waves below. The wind whipped her black dress against her legs and Claire leaned into it stubbornly.

She let her gaze drift along the rocky shore. At the end of a long dock some distance away, a sleek powerboat rocked up and down on the waves. Even from where she stood, Claire could see that it was expensive, probably worth more than the Wild Rose earned in six months. Frowning, she looked away. A man in a belted raincoat stood on the terrace above the dock where the boat was tied. He was watching her with binoculars.

"Don't worry, I won't steal your pretty boat," she muttered. With a grumpy sigh, she turned to retrace her steps.

She was honest enough to admit that it was more than Trelawney's funeral that had depressed her; she knew her mood was largely Hank's fault. Or to be even more honest, it was her own fault for wishing Hank hadn't left without a word. She wanted to know where he'd found the rum, and to discuss her ideas with him. She wanted to lock horns with him again and see the impudent challenge in his green eyes.

But that was idiotic, Claire scolded herself. She

picked her way back along the shore and mounted her bicycle again. If only to keep her mind off of Hank, she knew she must do something, take some positive action. Simply walking on the beach hadn't helped matters one bit, and the problem wasn't going to go away. She put her head down, rode back into town, and propped her bicycle up outside City Hall.

As Claire turned to go up the steps, Chief Handy walked out.

"Well, hello, Claire," he said with a smile. "What've you been up to today?"

Resentment wrinkled Claire's forehead and she looked down at her feet. There was sand on her shoes. "Nothing," she muttered.

"That's a load of applesauce, as you young people say," he teased her, looking down at her from the top step. "Didn't see you up on Burial Hill just now."

Claire adopted a lighthearted tone. "I didn't know I had to report to you," she said with a smile that did not reach her eyes.

"Report?" the man replied. "I just asked a friendly question. I know your mother worries when you're not home."

"My mother does not worry about me," Claire said more sharply. "She knows I can take care of myself, and I am surprised you have time to ask me questions when you've got yourself a murderer to find."

Handy's eyebrows nearly disappeared under his steely gray hair. "My, my, my," he said. He came slowly down the steps and looked Claire in the eyes. She lifted her chin, refusing to apologize.

"Claire, I sure do hope you aren't still running around playing girl-detective with your boyfriend," he said in a quiet voice.

Claire didn't let him see how the word "boyfriend" stung. She kept her eyes on the ground, mulishly silent, wishing desperately that her mother would send Handy packing.

"Claire?" Handy pressed. "I'm only concerned about your safety, you know. As you just pointed out, there's a murderer on the loose. I can't let you go poking into a hornets' nest. If something happened to you, why I'd never forgive myself."

She looked up into his face. Her hand itched to slap him, and she clenched her hands behind her. She didn't for a moment believe he was concerned about her safety. He was probably only concerned about being shown up by a girl, or about proving to Claire's mother what a fine, upstanding figure he was.

"Sir, you are not my father, and no matter what happens, you never will be," Claire said with a flash of anger. "It's none of your business what I do. And just because my mother likes you doesn't mean I have to."

He stared at her for a moment and then let out a low whistle. "You MacKenzie girls sure don't pull any punches. You're a lot like your Aunt Laura."

"I guess that means she never liked you, either," Claire said.

Chief Handy's face flushed a dark, angry crimson. "Well, I guess we know just where we stand, then. Good-bye, Claire." Handy strode past her and walked away.

Claire stood where she was, her mind spinning. She couldn't bear the thought of Handy becoming her stepfather, living at the Wild Rose, acting as though he owned the place. In her most secret heart, she wondered if he only pursued her mother to get his hands on the Wild Rose, if after giving up the Ship he was looking to acquire the MacKenzies' legacy. She closed her eyes, ashamed of how her thoughts betrayed her mother.

Then, overhead, the approaching drone of an airplane called Claire out of her blue fog. She squared her shoulders and ran up the steps and into the building. The door over the town clerk's office tinkled as she went inside.

"Well, hello there," said Mr. Chesnut, the clerk. He stopped typing and looked over the tops of his glasses at her. His high, domed forehead was lined with wrinkles.

"Mr. Chesnut, I wonder if I can look at some records," Claire said with a smile. "I want to know who bought the Ship from Chief Handy."

Mr. Chesnut sucked his teeth. "You just missed him, could've asked him yourself, Claire."

"I didn't see him," Claire lied, unwilling to admit that she couldn't bear to speak to Handy, let alone ask him for information. Besides, she knew she had a selfish desire to solve the case right under his nose, and the less he knew about her inquiries, the better. "Can't I just look at the records?"

The lines in Mr. Chesnut's forehead creased even more deeply. "Well . . . what do you want to know, for?"

Claire hesitated. She had never seen Chesnut at the speakeasy and didn't know if he knew about it. She gave the clerk a sheepish smile.

"Mr. Chesnut, I can confide in you, can't I?"

He nodded quickly. "By all means."

She lowered her voice. "Well, you know that Chief Handy is a bit sweet on my mother, and it's only natural that I want to look out for her welfare, and I thought if I saw what he got for the Ship, I'd have some notion of— you know."

"I see." Mr. Chesnut took off his glasses and rubbed the two dents on either side of his nose. A telephone tinkled faintly in an office down the hall. "Let me just see what I can find."

As he disappeared among aisles of shelving, Claire stood tapping her foot. Through the frosted glass window in the hall door, she could see the profile of a man standing on the other side. He didn't come in, but simply stood there, perfectly still. Claire leaned across the desk, silently urging Mr. Chesnut to hurry.

"Find anything?" she called impatiently.

"It's one of the oldest places in town," Chesnut replied from out of sight. His voice was muffled as he shifted ledgers and accordion files. "Hard to track these things down."

"But the sale was only last year, after Mrs. Handy

died," Claire pointed out. "Surely the records were updated then."

She glanced nervously over her shoulder: the figure at the door was gone, and its disappearance was even more unsettling, somehow.

Mr. Chesnut came slowly back to the desk, empty handed. "Out of luck. Those records have gone missing."

Claire looked at him, and he met her eyes unblinkingly.

"Missing?" she asked without hiding her skepticism.

"Missing," the clerk repeated. "Maybe you ought to ask the chief. That is, if you're so concerned about your ma," he added.

Something in his tone made Claire uneasy, and the unpleasant thought that Chesnut could be involved crept into her mind. She forced herself to smile.

"Well, a wild-goose chase, I guess. Maybe I will have to ask him, after all."

"Maybe. Now it's after one o'clock and I'm closing up for lunch, if you'll excuse me." Chesnut went back to his desk and sat down without another word.

Claire walked slowly out of the office and shut the door behind her. In the corridor, the light shone harshly from ceiling fixtures, drawing a white edge around the water fountain and pooling on the linoleum floor. There was no one in sight, although closed doors lined the hallway. Claire made for the outside door with the feeling that she was being watched. Her footsteps echoed on the tile walls, and she concentrated on keeping her pace steady.

When she reached the exit at last, she turned and glanced back.

Mr. Chesnut was watching her from the door of his office. Their eyes met, and then he turned and went back inside. The lock turned with a soft click like a gun being cocked.

Chapter Seven

On the steps in the sunshine, Claire paused to steady herself. Two old sailors from the funeral, Mr. Peavy and Mr. Bull, were walking down the sidewalk. Mr. Peavy smiled at her, showing the gaps in his teeth, and the two men continued on their way without speaking. At the filling station across the street, Mrs. Schirmer sat at the steering wheel of her Chrysler as Ed Loomis filled the tank. The activity in the street was no different than it was any other day, and yet Claire found every gesture and expression edged with menace.

Claire put her head down and walked her bicycle along the sidewalk, unwilling to look at anyone lest she see something she'd regret. More than anything, she wanted to cling to the belief that whoever was behind Tink's murder was from out of town: in other words, someone she hadn't known all her life. More than anything, she wanted to keep believing Tink's murderer was a stranger.

She turned the corner and almost ran into Bob. He instantly turned and fled.

"Bob MacKenzie!" Claire yelled. "Don't make me come after you!"

He skidded to a halt and reluctantly came back, hands in his pockets. "Guess there wasn't much point in running, was there?" he asked with an unapologetic grin.

"No, there wasn't, it was ridiculous," Claire replied. "So? Why aren't you in school? Fess up."

"Ma sent word to my teacher," Bob replied. "I've got a terrible headache and won't be in today."

As he stood there grinning at her, Claire felt anger and indignation steal through her. "Mother thinks you're in bed?"

Bob just laughed, watching her from the corner of his eye.

"Take that stupid grin off your face," Claire burst out suddenly. "You were disgusting last night and I'm sick of picking you up and taking you home. Where did you get the rum?"

Bob gaped at her, startled by her anger. "You know I was at the Ship," he began.

"Larry says they don't have rum at the Ship, and anyway, he wouldn't pour as much booze as you had in you last night," Claire said, her eyes hard. "Nobody would give a kid that much liquor."

"I'm not a kid," Bob said with sudden passion.

"Yes, you are. And you're a spoiled brat, too," Claire replied. "Where did you get it?"

Bob drew himself up. "I'm no snitch, Claire," he said haughtily. "I'm surprised at you."

"You're surprised at me?"

Claire put one hand over her eyes. Her own head was aching, and she hated sounding so shrill. "Bob, go to school," she pleaded.

"Well, I will, if you promise not to tell why I felt like such a dog this morning," Bob said.

Claire sighed. "No, I won't snitch on you."

"You know, you used to be a lot more fun, Sis," Bob added, sounding very aggrieved. "Why don't you loosen up, you look like you're going to a funeral."

"I have been to a funeral," Claire reminded him.

He had the grace to blush. "Oh, right. Well, then, in Tink's honor, why not take a drink now and then?"

"You're drinking enough for three people, these days," Claire told him.

"Just trying to have a good time."

"But Bob, it's *not* a good time," Claire said with a pleading look. "Not anymore."

Bob gazed blankly at her. His face was pale and unhealthy looking, and his eyes were red-rimmed. "I'm having the time of my life," he said.

"You can't be serious."

"Obviously no one can be as serious as you," Bob said, and walked away.

Claire watched him scuff along the sidewalk. Perhaps she had been more fun once, she admitted. But finding a man murdered could sober the liveliest soul. It dampened her spirits even more to know that she had been so affected.

Ahead of her in the near distance, the Cape Ann bus ground its way down a steep, hilly street in low gear. It rounded the corner with a belch of smoke, and pulled up in front of Curly's Drug Store. The door squeaked open and Hank jumped out, hat in hand. Her grip tightened on the handlebars.

"Hank!"

The rumbling of the bus engine drowned out her voice, and luckily Claire caught herself before she ran forward. She hung back, biting her lip. He had withheld an important clue from her and gone off without leaving any message. It still stung. But as she stood uncertainly by her bicycle he turned and saw her, and the smile on his face jolted Claire's heart.

"You came to meet me! How did you know?" he called. He swung his jacket over his shoulder and came toward her with a delighted smile.

"I didn't," Claire replied unsteadily. "I have no idea where you went and had no idea when you'd be back."

"Then it's just my lucky day." Hank laughed. "I couldn't wait to get back, I've got so much to tell you."

"Oh, I can hardly believe my good fortune," Claire said with a chilly smile.

"Me, neither," Hank said cheerfully. "I think I'm onto something."

She turned toward Front Street, and as he fell into step beside her he took the bicycle. Claire relinquished it without thanks, still angry that he made no apology for disappearing and angry with herself for being so shaken by his return.

"So where did you go?" she asked in a tight voice.

"Boston. The Federal Building." Hank's green eyes were bright with excitement. "A pal of mine works there, Joe Tucci."

"As what, the elevator boy?"

Hank let out a short laugh. "Not exactly. He's FBI. I thought he could help us out."

Claire looked away, frowning. They had almost reached the Wild Rose. "I don't know why you need to bring outsiders into this," she muttered.

"Say, hold on a minute." Hank took her arm and turned her to face him. "What's eating you? I've been in town five minutes and I'm in trouble already."

"I still think there are outsiders behind this mess," she said, trying to believe her own words. "I don't know why we need to bring in more."

"That's all it is?" Hank asked sharply. "That's the only reason you're giving me the high hat?"

Claire lowered her eyes. She knew she was blushing. "Yes," she lied.

"Well, if that's what's bothering you, maybe I ought to clear out. I guess I qualify as an outsider, too."

"No!" Claire opened the gate and walked into the garden. She paused for a moment, her head bowed as she reminded herself to think of what mattered and put aside her injured pride for Kitty's sake and for Bob's. Feeling sorry for herself wasn't useful at all.

"Hank, where did you get that bottle of rum in your closet?" she asked quietly.

Hank was silent. She raised her eyes to look at him, and he ran one finger under his collar. He was wincing.

"Hank?"

"Oh, I wasn't going to tell you," he said with a sigh. "I took it from your brother last night. He was behind the Ship with it, drinking in the alley. It looked like he was trying to get the whole thing down in one swallow."

Heat rushed into Claire's face and then ebbed away. "Thanks," she said with difficulty.

"He seems like a nice kid."

"He is." Claire sighed.

"Were you hoping maybe I'd confess to being the evil mastermind behind the rum smugglers?" Hank asked. "Me with my pal Tucci, the G-man?"

Claire shrugged one shoulder. "I didn't know that until just now. And besides, haven't you ever heard of corrupt cops?"

"She's such a cynic," Hank said, shaking his head and propping the bicycle against the fence. "What a pity in one so young and fair."

"Look," Claire said with a rueful laugh. "I'm sorry I snapped at you but it's been a trying day, so far—I had to go to Tink's funeral, and it was so pitiful. Can we start over again? Please?"

Hank smiled. "Sure."

Claire held out her hand. "Good afternoon, Mr. Logan. How are you today?"

Still smiling, Hank shook her hand. "Very well, Miss MacKenzie. I've been to Boston."

"And what did you learn there?"

Hank kept hold of her hand. "I learned that I wanted to get back here as fast as I could," he said, steadily meeting her eyes. His hand was warm around hers.

"You did?"

"You bet I did," Hank said, breaking away. He sat in garden chair with his hat on his knee. "I think we're onto something, here, Claire. Ever hear of a rum row?"

Claire tried to switch the direction of her thoughts as she sat in another chair. "No," she faltered.

"Joey has," Hank said, eagerly leaning forward and running one hand through his hair. "And he told me how it works. Somebody bankrolls a ship to sail for Canada or the islands, fills it up with hooch, and brings it back just beyond the three-mile territorial limit where the feds can't touch 'em. The bounding main is *wide* open, Claire, and there's nothing anyone can do about it."

"But what then?" Claire prompted him.

"Then a bunch of smaller boats go out there and pick up a load of rum and run it back in. It's easy for them to disappear on this coastline, as easy as it was a hundred and fifty years ago."

Claire's mind was racing. "Fishing boats, for instance."

Their eyes met, and at the same time they both said, "*Kittiwake.*"

"I think we can assume Trelawney was making pickups on the rum row," Hank said. "But he must have been

100

drinking too much of the hooch, or maybe he was getting a little too talkative or greedy, who knows? It's a gold-mine business, and whoever's running it probably got tired of worrying about the poor chump so they decided to bump him off."

"Poor chump," Claire repeated. She put her chin in her hands, following her train of thought. "And rich boss. If it is a gold mine, whoever's running things must be pretty rich."

"Anybody around here rich?" Hank asked lightly. "Let's go arrest 'em. If there's one thing I won't tolerate it's a rich man. It's purely the principle of the thing that riles me. When you're a penniless hack like me, you've got to believe there's something sinful about a rich guy. It soothes the ego, if you know what I mean."

While Hank rambled sarcastically, Claire was remembering her walk out on Marblehead Neck, and the posh summer homes there. She was also remembering the sleek, fast powerboat and the man watching over it with binoculars. The word "rich" was tickling her memory, and she looked up suddenly at Hank.

"That fellow Swenson looks pretty rich," she said.

"I'll say."

Claire studied his face. "I saw you with him last night."

"Sure, at the bar when you came into the Ship," Hank said, sitting back in the chair.

She shook her head slowly and kept her hands steady on the arms of her chair. "Later, too. Outside."

Hank looked at her blankly, and then his face relaxed

101

into a smile and he fished a pack of cigarettes from his pocket. "Oh, sure. Now I remember. I asked him for a light."

He bent his head as he lit a match, cupping the flame carefully, although there was no breeze in the sheltered garden. Claire watched him in silence, her heart thudding with sudden suspicion. He spent longer than necessary over the task.

But then he looked up again with his lopsided grin and Claire realized she was only letting the mood of the day lead her astray. She let out a small sigh and relaxed in her chair.

"So, let's hear what you've been doing today." Hank crossed ankle over knee and watched her through cigarette smoke. "If you weren't coming to meet me at the bus stop, you were doing something else."

"Clever deduction."

Hank loosened the knot of his tie. "Reporter's instincts," he said, tapping his temple with one finger.

Claire laughed and knew that she was happy, happy to be with Hank, happy to have someone she could talk to, happy to have him tease her as he did. She laughed from pure relief, knowing that Hank was one person in Marblehead she could safely hold above suspicion. He was a flirtatious scoundrel, and she knew she had to be on her guard lest she lose her heart. But Claire couldn't stay angry with him, didn't want to be angry with anyone. She had had enough of that for one day.

"I had a run-in with Handy," Claire said, rolling her

eyes. "He thinks he can boss me around and asked in that oh-so-patronizing way of his if I'm still playing detective."

Hank grinned. "Something tells me you don't much care for our good police chief."

"Oh, he makes me want to scream," Claire said. "I'm sure he intends to marry my mother, and the thought of that man living in my house . . ."

"Maybe your mother does intend to marry him," Hank said with a shrug. "But I have to say, you're a little hard on the guy."

Claire slumped down in her chair, stretched out her legs and crossed her ankles. She sighed. "Oh, I just can't help it. I don't suppose we could pin the murder on him? That would be one way of getting rid of him." She smiled crookedly at her own wild imagination.

Hank was gazing down at Claire's legs. He looked up slowly and grinned. "I'm sorry, what were you saying?"

"Nothing," Claire muttered, sitting upright and smoothing down her black skirt. She was blushing.

"Mourning becomes you," Hank said.

"I can only say I hope you won't get to see me in it again," Claire replied.

"Might be worth a couple more murders," Hank said, looking innocently at the sky.

Claire repressed a smile. "You're too much, Logan. As I was saying, I thought I'd look up the records on the Ship. I couldn't find out last night who actually owns the place now, so I thought I'd take a look at the deed."

"And?"

"And nothing," Claire said wryly. "Mr. Chesnut—the clerk—couldn't find anything."

"Do you think he was giving you the runaround on purpose?" Hank asked.

Claire frowned. "Mmm, I don't *think* so . . . And besides, he's from a very old Marblehead family. The Chesnuts have lived here for ages."

Hank quirked one eyebrow. "Do you really think Trelawney was the kind of guy to work for someone who *wasn't* from an old Marblehead family?"

"Well, n-no," Claire said slowly. "I realize there has to be at least one local person tied up in this. But it could be a summer person, someone with a house on the Neck, for instance. That would make him somewhat local."

"It couldn't possibly be anybody who's really from here," Hank said, calmly observing the red tip of his cigarette.

She raised her chin. "We just agreed that this business is making somebody a lot of money. The biggest money in this town is out on the Neck, not stuffed in the town clerk's mattress."

"All right, Claire," Hank said. "It's the big bad outsiders."

"Knock it off," she growled, smiling in spite of herself. "But listen, I went out to the Neck today, just for a walk. And I saw a very interesting boat."

"Just how interesting was it?"

"Extremely interesting," Claire said, becoming more excited the more she considered the possibilities. "A fast boat. An expensive boat."

Hank clapped one hand to his forehead in mock astonishment. "Not—a *rumrunner's* boat!"

Claire laughed. "I don't know," she admitted. "But I can't imagine they're relying too much on old lugs like the *Kittiwake*. Even if the freighters are out of reach, the boats bringing the stuff in must have to be pretty fast to dodge the coast guard."

"How many fast boats do you think are out there on the Neck?"

"I don't know for certain, but quite a few, I would guess," Claire said, crossing her legs and leaning back in her chair. She smiled serenely at Hank, who gave her a questioning look.

"Is there something else?" he asked. His smile made Claire's heart race.

"Well . . ." she began in a lazy drawl. "There may be quite a few boats out there, but I wonder how many of them are being guarded by men with binoculars."

Hank sat forward. "What?"

"I doubt he was watching the coast for U-boats," Claire said complacently. "I think we should go out there and take a little look."

"Claire," Hank said with an appraising look. "I think I agree."

Chapter Eight

Claire took the last of the dinner dishes into the kitchen. "I'm going out, Mother," she said, taking off her apron and combing out her hair with her fingers. "There's just Mr. Felice left in the dining room, and I think he's fallen asleep over his coffee."

Mrs. MacKenzie gave Claire a bright look. "Going to the pictures, dear?"

"No," Claire replied. "I'm just going out for a walk. I won't be late."

She let herself out the door into the garden. Hank was leaning against the side of the house, one foot hitched back on the wall behind him, but he pushed away as she came out. His cigarette made a red arc as he tossed it aside. The sky was deepening to purple behind his head.

"Ready?" Hank asked.

"Yes," Claire said, leading the way to the fence where her bicycle still stood. "Do you know how to ride someone on the handlebars?"

"Studied it in school. Got excellent marks, too."

Claire laughed. "All right, but if we crash—"

"Do you dare to doubt my abilities?" he asked, grabbing the bicycle and straddling it. "Hop on up there, Miss MacKenzie."

With another laugh, Claire hitched up her skirt and settled herself on the handlebars with her feet on the front fender. Hank pushed off, wobbling slightly. "You'll have to navigate, because I can't see a thing," he warned.

"It's not *that* dark, yet," Claire said.

"That's not the problem," Hank teased her. "There's a girl in the way and I can't take my eyes off her."

She faced forward, smiling into the wind. He was a scoundrel, without doubt. Houses rushed by, their yellow windows a blur in the twilight, and she could feel his breath on the back of her neck.

"Take this left, and try not to drive us into the ocean," she called over her shoulder.

"And miss getting the biggest scoop of the year? Don't you worry. If I break this story, it'll make my career. We're going to blow this thing wide open."

Claire grabbed for balance as the bicycle swerved down a hill. "Let's not use too much dynamite at once," she cautioned. "We don't want to hurt any innocent bystanders."

"Don't worry!" Hank said confidently.

Claire glanced back at him. She was worried. Marblehead was her town, and she knew everyone in it. People had families, friends, reputations. Claire wanted to tread carefully, and she would do what she could to keep anyone from getting caught in the cross fire. But she suspected Hank wouldn't bother to take such pains. For the first time, she was uncomfortably aware how different their motives were for tracking down Tink's murderer.

"Just don't do anything else without telling me first," she warned.

He laughed. "So you were sore about me leaving this morning! I can read you like a book, MacKenzie. Hang on!"

They swooped down another hill and then out toward the Neck. The wind sweeping across the spit from ocean to harbor buffeted the bicycle, and Claire had to concentrate on not falling off. The wheels made a quick clickety click as Hank pedaled out onto the Neck.

"Let's get out to the beach here," she said.

They coasted to a stop and Claire hopped off. The water was luminous at their backs. In the deepening night, the ocean was huge and wet all around them, a vast murmuring presence. A gentle surf shushed against the dark sand, and far off in the dark, the lights of freighters passed on their way to Europe and Canada.

"From here we can climb along the shore," Claire said, extending one slim arm to point to the water's edge. "The houses we want are on the ocean side. They're the most likely ones, with docks that can't be seen from town. I think the house I saw today is a good place to start, but we should try to find some other possibilities, too."

The breeze tossed Claire's short hair around her cheeks, and she turned this way and that to keep it out of her eyes. Hank stood in front of her and brushed it back with both hands.

"Did anyone ever tell you you're a remarkable girl, Clair-de-lune?" he murmured, his hands on either side of her face.

Claire let her breath out slowly. "Did anyone ever tell you you are very charming, Logan? Or do they assume you know that already?"

His teeth gleamed in the darkness, and he caught one of her hands and pressed it between his. "Hmm, just as I thought. You're still punching without gloves on."

Claire yanked her hand away. "Are you after a scoop, or aren't you?"

"Yes," he said.

"Then let's go." Claire struck out across the yielding sand, her heart pounding. She knew she was dangerously close to falling for Hank Logan, and she wasn't sure she wanted to. His charm was almost too effortless, and he had an unnerving effect on her knees. But most importantly, he was only passing through and would be gone as soon as he had his story. He was ambitious and would be off after the next hot scoop when this one was done. Charming and interesting men had stayed at the Wild Rose before, and Claire knew they always left. She had guarded her heart carefully before this, and would continue to do so.

"It's dark as the inside of a cat out here," Hank said as he trudged along beside her. "It's a pretty lonely spot. You sure there are houses? I'm beginning to worry you're going to sandbag me and throw me to the fishes."

"Trust me," Claire replied drily. "They're just empty for the winter, that's all. Now be careful, this is where it gets rocky."

They didn't speak for some time as they scrambled over granite boulders in the dark. All the while, the sound of waves on their right reminded them not to lose their footing. Claire led the way carefully from rock to rock, skirting tidal pools. Once she put her hand on a slimy patch of seaweed and pulled back with a startled cry. But Hank was right behind her and touched her shoulder to steady her.

"It levels off up here," Claire said, and the wind blew her voice into the night.

In a few minutes they gained higher ground and they could feel turf beneath their feet. Inland, all was darkness, not a light showing. The breeze from the water sent shivers up Claire's back.

"How far is the house where you saw the boat and the nervous guy with the binoculars?" Hank asked.

"A little farther. The shore curves around a bit more."

"Lead on."

The walking was easier on the grass and they kept pace side by side. Claire tried not to think about Hank except as her fellow detective. But she felt as though every square inch of her skin was more sensitive than usual, as though she had some special new sense that was tuned to his presence and nothing else. She wondered if he could ever love her, then quickly brushed the thought from her mind.

As they made their way around a jutting curve, they

spotted a solitary light. Claire halted, one hand on Hank's arm to stop him.

"That's it," she said quietly.

The light was at the end of the dock she had seen earlier. But no boat was moored there, now. The damp wind hushed intermittently in their ears, and the waves rolled in from the ocean to surge against the pilings of the deserted dock.

"Are you sure this is it?" Hank asked.

"Positive."

He let out a low, exultant laugh. "How many people take boats out at night? They must be out on rum row right now. This is it, Claire."

Claire shivered. "Maybe."

"The place is dark," he observed. "Let's take a look."

He struck out across the lawn, which rose toward a house silhouetted against the deep purple sky. Claire followed, her nerves jumping. Near the house, far from the luminous ocean, the darkness was deeper, and as they stepped onto a flagstone terrace, Claire's ghostly reflection walked toward her in a French window. Hank strode forward without hesitation, as bold as he had been on the *Kittiwake*.

"Doesn't anything make you nervous?" Claire asked. She hugged her arms around herself, shivering. "I can hardly get my breath, I'm so jumpy."

"The only thing around here that takes my breath away is you," he said, rattling a doorknob.

Her heart lurched with disappointment. He must have used that a hundred times, in just the same offhand tone. It was a line for the hatcheck girl at a nightclub, the usherette at a movie house—and the waitress in a seaside hotel. She felt like a fool for hoping he might ever really care for her.

"Let's check around the front of the house," Hank said as he tried another door. "We're not making much progress, here. I'd love to get a look inside."

"Are you really going—" Claire tensed, straining to hear through the wind. "Something's coming."

"What?"

"I think I heard an engine," Claire whispered. "A boat."

They stood motionless until the wind died for a moment and they could both hear it clearly. Instantly, they began to run back the way they had come, racing over the springy grass. Out on the water, a searchlight switched on and beamed toward the dock. Claire's heart stuck in her throat as the light moved back and forth. Hank grabbed her hand.

"Don't move," he whispered.

Then the searchlight began moving toward where they stood, and just before it reached them, Hank pulled Claire into his arms and began to kiss her.

For a moment, she was too astonished to think. Hank tightened his arms around her and moved to kiss her cheek and her hair, and Claire forgot that they were being pinned by a spotlight.

"Lovers on the beach, make it look real," Hank whispered.

Claire leaned against him as he kissed her again, her

arms around his neck, her thoughts racing. It was real. She didn't have to pretend. "Oh, Hank."

"Hey!" an angry voice yelled across the waves. *"Beat it! You're trespassing!"*

Hank let go of Claire and shielded his eyes against the blinding glare. "Sorry!" he called. "Didn't know anyone was around."

Claire thought her knees would buckle, but she didn't know if she was terrified by the spotlight or swept off her feet by Hank. He took her arm and steered her quickly back down the beach.

"Just act natural," he muttered.

Claire couldn't speak. The spotlight on their backs stretched their shadows ahead of them on the grass, and she stumbled as they rounded the bend. Hank held her up, and helped her around a rough spot until they were out of the line of fire. As soon as they were sheltered, they stopped.

"Holy Toledo," Hank breathed. "That was a little close."

He sat down on a boulder, and Claire heard the rustle of a cigarette pack. A match flared briefly, lighting his face for an instant before the wind whipped it out. Claire stood rigid and trembling. She put her hand to her mouth. She could still feel his kisses there.

"Wish we could have seen what was in the boat," Hank said with a chuckle. "Jeez, I didn't figure they'd be so suspicious they'd rake the place with a searchlight before they docked."

"No, I didn't either," Claire whispered.

"Didn't seem like a big boat, though. I wonder how much he could carry?"

As he continued to speculate about the boat's cargo, Claire found herself wondering what had just happened. For a moment, she had kissed Hank as though she could pour herself into him, and he had done the same. Or so it had felt.

But now, standing in the chill wind, Claire began to fear that for Hank it had only been a good cover. The longer he talked without mentioning their kiss, the more Claire doubted there had been any meaning to it at all. She was grateful for the darkness. She thought she must be as pale as a ghost—and the biggest fool in the world.

"I've got to get back there and take a good look around," Hank continued in an excited voice. "I've got a good feeling, Claire. I think this could be the story of my career."

Claire felt sick. "I have to go home," she said.

"Oh, sure, it's getting cold. Let's go."

As they scrambled back along the shoreline to the bicycle, Hank kept up his excited chatter. He talked of his days in Chicago, and of close calls he had had with gangsters, and about surly editors and late nights and deadlines. Claire walked silently behind him, wishing he would stop talking. She wished she could slap his face, but she was too mortified.

"Oh, God," she whispered.

"I know what you mean," Hank said with a laugh. "We're getting close."

When they reached the beach at last, they heard a car

motoring toward the mainland from behind them. A pair of headlights swept down the road and passed them, and Claire caught a glimpse of gleaming fenders and chrome. The car sped toward town, and the sound of its engine faded away.

"What do you say we stop in at the Ship," Hank suggested as he picked up the bicycle. "I could use something to warm me up."

Claire didn't answer. She wondered how she could ride on the handlebars back to town, with Hank so close, so careless, his breath against her ear. He was wheeling the bicycle off the sand and onto the pavement, whistling cheerfully to himself. The danger had thrilled him. Claire followed him with stiff steps.

"Hey, Claire," Hank said in a more sober tone. He cleared his throat. "About what happened back there. Just so you know, I wasn't—"

"Oh, please don't bother to apologize," Claire broke in with cold formality. "Really, I completely understand exactly what it was. It was nothing. It meant nothing at all."

Hank was silent for a long moment. "I guess you understand everything very well," he said in a strange voice.

"Can we please go?" Claire said, close to tears. "I'm frozen."

"Claire—"

"If you don't want to ride me on the handlebars, I can walk," she added.

He cursed. "Get on."

With shaking hands, Claire pulled herself up onto the handlebars and tucked her skirt under her knees. Hank stood on one pedal, pushed the bicycle and swung his other leg over the seat. They rode into town in chilly silence.

Claire felt stunned. Hank had kissed her, and instead of being happy, she wanted to cry. When they reached the Ship at last she was almost too stiff with cold and misery to get off. She nearly fell as she hopped off beneath a streetlight, and Hank moved as though to help her, but then stopped himself. Claire steadied herself against the hood of a lavish Cadillac Phaeton parked at the curb and for a moment stood with her head bowed, letting the warmth of the car's engine steal into her hands.

"I'll just go on in," Hank said gruffly. He pulled his hat down over his eyes and went into the Ship without another word. At the door, he gave a mumbled greeting to someone coming out, and the door shut on him.

Claire slowly raised her eyes. Zeke Penworthy was standing on the doorstep, lighting a cigarette.

"Evening, Claire," he said.

"Hello, Zeke," she said in a dull voice.

She lowered her head again and absently gazed down at the front of the car she was leaning on. The way the Cadillac's polished fenders and chrome gleamed in the streetlight whispered in her ear.

"Who owns this car, do you know?" Claire asked Zeke softly.

Zeke blew two streams of smoke through his nostrils.

"You know him, that rich fellow with the white hair. Swenson."

Claire withdrew her hands from the car's warm hood. "Does Mr. Swenson own a house on the Neck?"

"Now that you mention it, I think he does," Zeke said.

"He comes here pretty often," Claire observed.

Zeke rubbed his nose. "So do lots of people. Your brother's here tonight, for instance. And your friend Kitty."

Claire swallowed hard. "Everybody seems to be here," she said bitterly. "Drinking and having a good old time."

The bouncer gave her a puzzled, apologetic look. "What are you doing out here on the sidewalk in the cold, Claire? Come on in, there's a boy from Newport with a cornet, and he sure can blow it."

"No," Claire said, looking up at the old frame building as she backed away. "I don't think I want to go in there tonight."

"What about that fellow you came with?" Zeke asked, jerking his thumb over his shoulder. "Want me to go get him?"

"No!" Claire shook her head, and pulled her sweater tighter around her shoulders. "If he notices I'm gone, tell him I went home."

Without waiting for Zeke's reply, Claire walked slowly away from the speakeasy. Her footsteps echoed against houses and shops as she passed down the street, and she made her way home more by habit than con-

117

scious plan. Sighing, she went through the garden of the Wild Rose and let herself in through the kitchen door.

Her mother and Chief Handy were sitting at the table. He was tucking into a large slice of apple pie, while Ellie MacKenzie worked at a splinter on the thumb of his other hand. Both of them looked around as Claire came quietly in.

"Had a nice walk?" Mrs. MacKenzie asked.

Claire noted that her mother's face was flushed with pleasure, and that the radio was tuned to a Chicago dance orchestra. She sighed again.

"It was fine," Claire said, and turned to pass through the kitchen to the hall.

"Did you go anywhere special?" Handy's voice was quiet in the peaceful kitchen.

Nonplussed, Claire looked back from the door. Her mother was still concentrating with needle and tweezers on Handy's thumb: she seemed oblivious to his attack on Claire's privacy. Claire turned a cold gaze on the police chief.

"Where did you go, Claire?" Handy repeated. He smiled.

"I'm not sure I know why it's any of your business," Claire said quietly. "This makes twice today you've asked me where I've been."

"But sweetheart," Mrs. MacKenzie spoke up. "He's just looking out for your welfare, that's all. It's only natural he should be concerned about you. It's a fatherly concern."

"No, it isn't," Claire insisted. She met her mother's

eyes. "I remember my father and Chief Handy is nothing like him. Have *you* forgotten?"

The color slowly faded from Mrs. MacKenzie's cheeks. "That was uncalled for."

Claire instantly regretted her words, and her heart twisted behind her ribs. "Oh, Mother, I—"

"Now, let's not get all riled up," Handy said easily. He met Claire's eyes. "All I asked was where you went. We've had a murder in town, and I'd like to know what you think you're doing out alone at all hours of the night. This town and everyone in it is my responsibility."

She stared at him. For the first time, he seemed not quite the boorish, patronizing incompetent Claire had always thought him to be. On the contrary, there seemed to be a degree of purpose and efficiency in his bearing that she'd never noticed before. He hardly looked like a man who had only been sitting and reading the newspaper, and Claire wondered if she had underestimated him. He might in fact be following the same leads she was, and be drawing the same conclusions.

"There's nothing to worry about," she said, slowly turning to look at her mother instead of Handy. "I wasn't alone. I went for a walk on the beach with Mr. Logan."

"Oh, Claire," Mrs. MacKenzie said. "Just the two of you in the dark? What were you thinking? Her good reputation is the most valuable possession a woman has."

"That's right," Handy agreed, giving Mrs. MacKenzie a proprietary look. He patted her hand and then glanced at Claire. "Listen to your mother. Stay home like a good girl."

Claire hunched her shoulders against a weight of helpless, sickening frustration. She'd always prided herself on having everything under control, on being able to manage.

But the night had proven to her that nothing was in her control. Not her mother. Not Handy. Not Hank. Nothing at all.

Chapter Nine

CLAIRE STOOD AT her bedroom window to watch the sun come up beyond the ocean. The eastern sky reddened and then burned to yellow, and she opened the window to let the cool, clear air wash over her. The breeze raised goose bumps on her skin, and Claire rubbed her arms, frowning into the sunrise.

She knew she must be as cool and clear as the morning was. She knew she must not let her feelings for anyone cloud her judgment. Except for her immediate family, Claire knew she must consider everyone a suspect.

Including Hank.

Claire hardened her heart and made herself repeat it. Hank was a suspect, too.

After all, what did she know of him but what he had chosen to tell? She knew no one who could vouch for him. He had arrived on the night of the murder and had left the Ship long before Claire found Tink's body. His answers were so smooth and plausible, his casual conversations with the mysterious Swenson so easily explained away. He claimed to have taken the bottle of rum from Bob, but how could she be sure that was true? He could be playing along with her just to keep her from learning anything important, could have called ahead to warn the owners of the powerboat that they were coming. By his own admission, he was familiar with the ways and means of gangsters and bootleggers—and for that matter, she had only his word that he was a reporter to begin with.

Claire shook her head, disgusted with her own gullibility. How many questions had he sidestepped with his charm and his flattery, and how many times had she lost her train of thought when she was with him, simply from looking into his green eyes?

"You idiot," she groaned, slamming the window shut. Her glance fell on the rumpled sheets of her bed, and a flush of shame raced up her back. She had dreamed of Hank in the night, dreamed of him kissing her.

But Hank was a suspect. So was Chesnut. So was anyone who wasn't in Claire's view at the Ship on the night of the murder. No one was above suspicion, as far as Claire was concerned. Swenson seemed a likely candidate for big-money backer, but had he pulled the trigger? Did he deign to dirty his cashmere coat or did he have a local hired gun to do the shooting?

She sat slowly on the edge of her bed, rubbing her thumbnail along her lips and frowning in concentration. She tried to imagine the weight of a gun in her hand, tried to imagine what it was like to pull a trigger.

Then, in her mind's eye she clearly saw the heavy

revolver Handy wore on his belt. She frowned, feeling strangely treacherous. Why not consider Handy a suspect, too? What better cover than being chief of police? And the more Claire let the idea develop, the more intrigued she became. Maybe he knew much more than anyone gave him credit for. Perhaps he knew very well what his old home had become, perhaps he was turning a blind eye, maybe even taking a little hush money. If he had been close to bankruptcy when he sold the Ship, he might be all the more willing to take a bribe. Perhaps that was why he was so concerned about Claire's snooping.

But the next moment, Claire knew she was just giving in to wishful thinking. The more she disliked Handy, the more determined she was to be fair and evenhanded. The fact that she had always mistrusted him did not make him an accomplice in a murder.

Claire left her bedroom, her bare feet noiseless in the passage. She ran past Bob's room and knocked on her mother's door.

"Are you awake, yet?" she whispered.

The door opened. Mrs. MacKenzie, in dressing gown and curlers, beckoned Claire in.

"Good morning, darling," she said, turning to the mirror and uncoiling her hair from the stiff metal rollers. She hummed under her breath, happy as she always was in the mornings.

Claire sat on the end of the big double bed and tucked her legs under her. She watched her mother's face in the mirror, trying to figure out what it was she wanted to say.

123

"I should be angry with you today," Mrs. MacKenzie began, dropping a hairpin into a cut-glass dish. "You were very rude last night when you came in."

"I know, Mother, I'm sorry," Claire replied. She smoothed the bedspread under her hand. "I didn't mean to hurt your feelings."

"Well, I forgive you, darling." Mrs. MacKenzie smiled at Claire through the mirror. "But I think you owe some-one else an apology, too."

Claire curled her toes in disgust. "You mean Chief Handy?"

"Yes, I can't think what got into you last night, Claire. He's—well he's very important to me, I think you're old enough to be told."

Claire groaned inwardly. "Mother, I know," she whispered. "I know."

"Well, then?"

"But how could you let him speak to me the way he did, Mother? He had no right."

"Of course he does!" Mrs. MacKenzie turned around, gesturing with her hairbrush. "He feels a responsibility to our family, and I'm very grateful to him for it. He wants to look out for you, and he knows Bob is a headstrong boy. Jack wants to take Bob under his wing."

"Then why doesn't he stop Bob from drin——" Claire stood up, frowning mulishly at the floor.

"From what?"

Claire crossed the room to the dresser, where a pho-tograph of her father in his U.S. Navy uniform sat among bottles of cologne and boxes of powder. He looked out at her with MacKenzie eyes, and the smile that she'd seen so often on Bob's face.

"Mother, did you ever ask Chief Handy who bought the Ship after Mrs. Handy died?" she asked.

"No, I didn't think it was my place to ask. If he wanted to tell me, I'm sure he would."

"I doubt it," Claire muttered.

"Why would he be mysterious about such a thing?" her mother scoffed. "Muriel Handy spent nearly every penny he had, and he just wasn't making the business thrive the way he had always taken such pride in doing. I'm not surprised that he wanted out, or that it's a painful subject for him."

"I just think it's odd that a Handy would let go of the Ship in the first place," Claire said in a low voice. In the face of her mother's sympathy for the man, Claire's determination to be fair had completely dissolved.

Her mother gaped at Claire for a moment and then laughed. She began brushing her hair with hard, brisk strokes, smiling at her reflection in the mirror. "Oh, Claire, don't tell me this is about that silly old feud be-- tween the Handys and the MacKenzies?"

"No!" Claire faced her mother. "No, I'm telling you I have a bad feeling about him. I don't trust him."

Mrs. MacKenzie shook her head with an indulgent laugh. "He's completely dependable, he has a good job, and he's a perfect gentleman—which is probably more than you can say for that Mr. Logan," she added sharply.

Claire blushed scarlet. "Mr. Logan has nothing to do with this conversation."

"I think he has everything to do with it," her mother retorted. "But I'm shocked to find that you're jealous of my friendship with Chief Handy."

"Jealous?" Claire's voice quavered. "Mother, I'm not jealous that you have a suitor. I'd be happy for you to be married again. But not to Chief Handy! I think he's crooked!"

"Claire, that's enough!" Mrs. MacKenzie grabbed Claire's wrists, her own face flushed with anger. "I won't hear any more of these reckless and childish slanders! Did your Aunt Laura tell you something against him?"

Claire shook her head. "No."

"I don't know what you have against him, then," her mother said. "You've never made any attempt to make friends with Jack. Frankly, I'm ashamed of you."

Claire pulled her arms out of her mother's grip. "I'm sorry you're ashamed of me," she said with difficulty.

"Not more than I am."

Claire left her mother's bedroom, breathing as hard as if she'd been running. Her eyes were blurred with tears, and she stumbled down the stairs with one hand clenching the banister. She paused at the bottom of the staircase, amazed that her life had become so painful in such a short period of time. The violence of Tink's murder seemed to be ricocheting off everything Claire loved. She was so confused she didn't know whom to suspect.

The front door opened, letting a flood of sunlight into the foyer. Claire winced and turned her face away from the brightness.

"Good morning," Hank said in a guarded tone.

His voice made her heart squeeze painfully inside her. "Morning," she replied.

She couldn't bring herself to look at him, wondering if he could be involved. As he walked slowly toward her, Claire clutched the banister until her knuckles turned white. She stood braced as though she stood in a high wind.

He stopped below her, and at last, she looked at him. "Where did you go when you left the Ship the night we met? Why did you leave?"

He quirked one eyebrow. "Am I being grilled?"

"Please tell me the truth," Claire whispered.

"I was tired and came back here to see if I could get a room," he said, frowning. "Claire, are you all right? You're as white as a sheet."

Claire looked at him searchingly, and slowly shook her head. She couldn't bring herself to really consider him as a suspect in the murder. He couldn't be.

"I—I've been thinking," she began.

"And?"

"And I think that Handy is—might be involved in this somehow," Claire whispered, sitting down on the bottom step.

He lounged against the banister, sending a cautious glance around the empty foyer. "Do you have some reason to suspect him, or are you just getting a head start on today's wishful thinking?"

She wrapped her arms around her knees. "I know I've got reasons to wish he did it. But I've always trusted my instincts before. I don't trust Handy. I don't like him."

"So it's got to be someone you don't like? Come on, Claire, don't be a sucker," Hank said. "Whether it's someone you like or don't like, or someone whose family has been around forever or who just moved here, we've got a responsibility to find out who it is."

Claire snapped her head up. "You don't give a damn who it is, all you care about is your story!"

"Why shouldn't I profit if I solve the case?" Hank asked.

"You?" Claire stood up, giving Hank a cold look. *"You* solve the case? I thought it was *we."*

"I like that! First you tell me to take a hike, then you get all huffy because I'm leaving you out! If that isn't *just* like a woman," Hank exclaimed.

"And you're just like any other man," Claire choked. "You can justify anything as long as you get what you want. You don't care who gets hurt."

"I'm *trying* to make sure you *don't* get hurt," Hank said angrily.

"Oh, of course, you're protecting me," Claire shot at him. "Like when you took that bottle from my brother and didn't tell me about it. I had a right to know!"

"Maybe I should have just let him keep it and let you take care of everything, since you're so all-fired determined to be the captain of this ship."

"I don't want to be captain, I just want to be partners, like you said," Claire said. "But you're so damned slippery and evasive all the time, I don't know who's side you're on."

128

Hank let out an ironic laugh. "Oh, now I get it. You do think I'm one of the bad guys. Beaut-i-ful."

Claire couldn't answer. They glared at one another for a long, silent moment, and then she turned and fled down the corridor, straight-arming through the kitchen door. It banged shut behind her, and she burst through the back door to the garden, fighting tears. She wished she had never thought to find Trelawney's killer.

Claire paced back and forth across the dewy grass, ignoring her wet shoes. She bent to break off the head of a withered chrysanthemum, but the stringy stem fought her and she yanked harder until she uprooted the whole plant. Dirt and petals sprinkled onto her dress.

"Damnit!" She threw it away from her with an angry sob.

The clump landed with a thud near the shed, and she heard a groan. Frowning, Claire followed the sound, parting the overgrown grass by the fence until she came across her brother, asleep in the wet weeds beside the old cow shed.

"Bob!"

He lifted one hand to rub his eyes and let out another groan as Claire knelt beside him.

"Bob, did you sleep here all night?" she gasped, shaking him awake.

With a moan, Bob pushed himself upright and leaned against the shed. His face was puffy and pale, one cheek creased with the impression of grass and sticks.

"Not all night," he muttered, licking his lips with difficulty. He sounded still drunk, and when he opened his eyes, Claire was sure he was. His eyes were bloodshot and unfocused, and the sunlight seemed to hurt him.

"Bob, how can they let you get like this?" Claire said in a tearful voice.

He squinted to see her. "Who?"

"Larry Penworthy and everyone else at the Ship."

"Wasn't at the Ship," Bob slurred.

Claire fought not to cry. "Yes, you were, Zeke told me you were there."

He raised one finger. "But just f'r a while 'n then went somewheres else. And don't ask where!" he added huffily. "A gen'lman never tells."

"Does Hope know you get falling down drunk every night?" Claire asked.

Bob's chin trembled. He clutched at Claire's arm and struggled to speak.

"What?" Claire said. "What is it?"

Bob shook his head, and a tear ran down his face. "God, she wants t' give it away," he brought out at last. "Claire you gotta—you gotta help me."

Claire felt as though the wind had been knocked out of her. "Is Hope going to have a baby?"

"Don' tell anyone. Please." Bob choked back a sob. "I didn't mean for it to happen. I—I love Hope."

"Then marry her," Claire said.

"I want to. But Hope says she won't get hitched to a —a—"

"A drunkard," Claire finished for him.

Bob nodded, fresh tears pouring from his eyes.

"I can't blame her," Claire said. "Neither would I.

130

Now if you want my help—my help to get Hope to change her mind—then *you* better straighten up."

The spring on the screen door creaked, and the door slapped shut. Claire looked over her shoulder to see their mother coming hesitantly across the garden.

"What is it, Claire? What are you looking at?" Mrs. MacKenzie called.

Claire couldn't answer. Her mind was reeling. She stood up stiffly as their mother came through the garden, picking her way through the wet grass until she saw Bob.

"Oh, my lord! What happened?" Mrs. MacKenzie quailed. She hurried to Bob's side and felt his forehead. "You're burning up! I knew you were coming down with something. Oh, poor baby!"

Claire backed up, drawing a harsh breath. "He's not sick! He's not sick, Mother, can't you see that?"

"What?"

Claire pressed both hands to her face and then flung them outward in pain. "He's drunk! He's only a kid, but he's so drunk he can't even stand up!"

"What are you talking about?" Mrs. MacKenzie asked, her eyes wide. "He's not drunk, of course he's not drunk, he's taken a chill."

"Because he passed out in the garden!" Claire shouted.

"Keep your voice down, Claire! This is outrageous!"

Claire met her mother's eyes. "Why don't you get the upright and dependable Chief Handy to look after him?"

On the ground, Bob giggled again. "He's 'pendable, all right."

Claire felt suddenly cold. She bent down and took Bob's chin, forcing him to look at her. "Is it him?" she demanded. "Is Handy the one who gets you the rum?"

"Claire! How dare you?" Mrs. MacKenzie pushed Claire's hand away from Bob, and put her arm around his shoulders. "How can you be so vicious?"

Claire shook her head in disbelief. "If I'm right, vicious doesn't begin to describe what Handy is doing."

"Get out!" Mrs. MacKenzie cried shrilly. "Don't come back until you're ready to apologize!"

Claire stared at her mother.

"Get out!" Mrs. MacKenzie cried again, hunching over Bob. "Get out! Get out!"

Chapter Ten

CLAIRE RAN THROUGH the garden, catching herself on the corner of the house and trying not to cry.

She wouldn't cry: she refused to cry. She drew a deep breath and walked around the corner and saw Hank standing motionless by the door. On his face was such an expression of pity that Claire thought she would burst into tears.

"Claire, I'm so sorry—"

"No," she growled, brushing past him and struggling with the gate. She wrenched open the latch and ran into the street.

"Claire, wait!"

She ignored him, keeping her head down and running as fast as she could through town. Behind her, Claire heard Hank's footsteps as he came after her.

Without stopping, she yelled, "Don't follow me! Get away from me!"

Claire wiped a tear from her eye with a rough gesture, and took the path that led up Burial Hill. Dead leaves scurried across her way as she toiled up the hill, catching hold of lichened gravestones to pull herself up the steep track. She struck off the path at an angle, the quicker to reach the top. The short grass was smooth and dry underfoot, and all around Claire the dead of Marblehead lay beneath the turf. There was a fresh grave near a crowd of by-gone Trelawneys, off to one side like a poor relation. A bouquet of white chrysanthemums on the mound was already withering brown, the petals scattered like dirty snow.

"Claire, slow down!"

Claire spun around, almost losing her balance on the slippery grass of the hill. "I told you not to follow me!"

With growing exasperation, she turned to clamber up and over a rock outcropping. Claire was short of breath, almost dragging herself up to the summit against the breeze. She heard him huffing and puffing behind her, and she turned to confront him with a look of outrage.

"For the last time!"

Her feet slid out from under her, and Hank lunged to help her, but he slipped on the smooth grass, as well. Both of them collapsed into ungainly heaps on the ground.

For a moment, Claire thought she would scream with indignation, but when she looked at Hank rubbing his bruised knee, a laugh bubbled up inside her, instead. She shook her head.

"You are the most infuriating person in the world," she complained. "I told you and told you not to follow me."

Hank pulled himself upright, dusting off his knees, and reached to give her a hand. "I'm stubborn."

Claire regarded his outstretched hand and then raised her eyes to his face. "I really did want to be alone," she said soberly.

"I know," Hank said. "But you're alone too much."

"Oh, there you go again," Claire said. She still hadn't taken his hand. "What makes you so sure you know everything about me?"

He shrugged and sat back down on the grass beside her. Before them, a wide prospect stretched to the horizon, and the wind blew fresh in their faces. He squinted against the bright sky.

Claire watched him impatiently. "Well?"

"We're alike in so many ways, Claire, that's how I know," he answered.

She snorted. "I suppose that's meant to flatter me?"

"Not at all, I'm not such an ideal specimen," Hank said drily. "But I know you. You want everyone to believe you're so tough, so capable, that nothing gets under your skin. Nothing takes you by surprise, nothing shocks you, no problem is more than you can handle. God forbid you ever admit you can use some help, or let anyone see that you're lonesome or blue."

Claire hugged her knees and fought a shiver. "Well . . ." she faltered. "It's true. I can manage on my own. I have to."

"Claire, come on!" Hank shook his head. "You know it's not true. You know it's not," he repeated.

With a sigh, Claire rested her cheek on her knees and

watched the wind blowing Hank's hair back from his fore-head. Inside her, something yearned to give way, stop fighting. She sighed again more deeply.

"Hank, if I start feeling sorry for myself, you'll have a whimpering idiot on your hands."

"Whimper away," Hank said, smiling kindly. "I'm up to it. You can't keep it locked inside forever. Go ahead and snivel."

She laughed, but it was close to a sob. "No."

He touched her arm with a blade of grass. "Claire, listen. You've got a tough life here, don't let anybody tell you you don't. People in town have talked about the Wild Rose, they say what a terrific spot it was before your father died, and before Prohibition sent everyone underground."

"Don't," Claire whispered.

"And I can see your mother is more than happy to leave all the decisions and hard choices to you, and your brother obviously isn't any help. He starts each day with a hangover and ends it falling down drunk."

"Don't, please," Claire said, squeezing her eyes shut.

"Your mother is in such a sweat to chuck her responsibilities, she'll give them all to that buffoon, Handy."

Claire shook her head. Her heart was pounding in her ears.

"Your family knows you're stronger and braver than most people, and they know you'll carry your own burdens and theirs, too," Hank continued vehemently. "And you do it day after day."

"Stop it!" Claire pressed both hands against her mouth, trying not to cry. Her family had never needed her more, and she had never felt less able to help. The breeze pressed against her back, and suddenly, Claire lost the battle. "I'm so tired," she whispered.

She buried her face in her hands and let Hank pull her into his arms. Deep sobs shook her as she pressed her face against his shirt, and she cried harder than she had in years. She cried for her father and the Wild Rose, and for her mother and brother—for the Trelawneys, and for herself. Claire didn't know how long she cried, but Hank held her tight the entire time.

"I've got you, I'm here," Hank murmured, rubbing her shoulder as her sobs quieted. "How about a hanky?"

Claire struggled upright and gaped at him. "A Hanky?" she repeated in a teary, bewildered voice.

He dug in his pocket and pulled out a handkerchief, and Claire stared at it for a puzzled moment. "Oh, a *hanky*, thank you," she sniffled as she took it and wiped her eyes.

"What did you think I meant?" he asked, brushing a damp lock of hair from her cheek.

Claire sighed. She already felt much better. "Oh, I don't know. Why are you always right? I hate that."

"I'm not always right," Hank replied, settling back against a gravestone and smiling at her. His eyes were warm and kind. "But I had a feeling you needed a good cry."

"Well, I guess I did." Claire said, wadding up the damp handkerchief in her fist. She felt light and tired, but not unhappy, as she gazed out at the ocean. "I suppose you'll get sore if I apologize for breaking down. But after all, it's your fault, you monster."

He let out a laugh. "Claire, you're really something, you know that? And that's not just idle flattery," he added hastily. "I may be glib sometimes, but give me a chance to be sincere, once in a while."

"Once in a while," Claire allowed. She couldn't help smiling at him. He made her happy, and she couldn't deny it. Her smile widened as they looked at one another. "So, we're a lot alike, huh?"

"I think so," Hank said.

"So all those things you said about me, I guess you mean they apply to you, too?" Claire asked.

"Maybe," Hank replied. He was smiling guardedly, his green eyes gleaming.

Claire was beginning to enjoy herself. She sat up on her knees and folded her arms. "So, Mr. Logan, you're not as hard-boiled as you like to seem, either? Not quite the tough-as-nails reporter?"

"Oh, I'm plenty tough, believe you me," Hank said.

"And nothing ever gets under your skin? And you never let anyone see if you get lonesome or blue?" she continued.

He grinned. "What are you going to do, try to make me cry?"

"I should, you probably need a good cry," Claire muttered.

Hank laughed again and jumped to his feet. "Claire, I haven't been lonesome or blue since I got here—and you can pretend you don't know why, if you want. That's fine.

After all, two tough customers like us shouldn't go sloshing our deepest secrets all over the place like a couple of weepy drunks."

Claire smiled up at him. "No, we could never do that."

"I'll tell you what else," he said. "I'm so far from being lonesome or blue that I think it's time for a day off."

"A day off?" Claire echoed.

"Yeah, it's what they call a day when you don't work," Hank replied. "Ever heard of it?"

Claire made a skeptical face. "Well, it seems to me I had one, once . . ."

Hank quirked one eyebrow. "Be serious. When was the last time you played hooky and just went to a matinee or on a picnic?"

"I honestly don't remember," Claire said, startling herself. She gazed out to sea and watched a distant ship make its slow progress against the ocean. From where she sat, the ship seemed almost miraculously free and cut off from the world.

"Then this is your day," Hank said decisively. "You name it, we'll do it. Whatever you want, Claire. The sky's the limit."

Claire tapped her chin with one finger while she thought. "You know what I'd love to do more than anything?"

"I'm dying to know," Hank replied with a lopsided grin.

"It's silly, but what I really want to do is go dancing."

He cocked his head to one side. "In the middle of the day? Where are we going to find a joint open at this time?"

Claire shrugged. "I told you it was silly. But you asked."

"And I told you we'd do whatever you want," Hank said. He rubbed his hands together, frowning. "All right, you sit tight. I'll be back before you can say Charleston."

Before Claire could answer, Hank began scrambling back down the steep slope, slipping and running until he was out of sight. Claire let out a startled laugh. She couldn't guess what he thought he was up to, but she was touched anyway. Smiling, she lay back on her elbows and gazed out over the treetops and chimneys of town toward the Atlantic. She steadfastly refused to look at the harbor or the Neck or to think about the murder. And soon, she knew, she would have to decide how she could help her brother and Hope. But for a while, anyway, she was going to stop worrying at her problems like a dog with a bone and simply relax.

The burying ground was peaceful, the sun warm, the sky the clear, deep blue that only appears in late September. Tall, unclipped grasses sprouted close by the headstones like tufts of hair, and crickets chirped within them. Claire closed her eyes against the sun, and her eyelids burned a warm red. She was almost tempted to go to sleep, but she was content to lie there, just daydreaming, for several minutes. Then a chickadee sang "see-see-see!" and Claire rolled over to watch its acrobatics among the spiny canes and red hips of a wild rose.

"See-see-see!" it chirped again.

Claire laughed. "I'm watching."

A blue jay landed on the grass nearby, cocked its head toward Claire, bobbed its tail and let out a raucous "Jee-ah!"

"Aren't you the bold one," Claire said. She followed the jay with her eyes as it flew away and saw Hank toiling back up the hill with something in his arms.

Claire smiled. "Speaking of bold," she murmured to herself, and a gull winging overhead let out a squawk like laughter.

"What've you got?" Claire asked, sitting up and shielding her eyes against the sun with one hand.

"A dance hall!" Hank called back. As he climbed nearer, Claire could see he was carrying a Victrola, the flaring bell of its speaker tucked under his arm. Claire watched in astonishment as he set it down on the grass at her feet.

"Where did you come up with that?" she asked.

"I have my ways," Hank replied, opening the case and fitting the bell into place. On the inside of the lid were several records, gleaming black in the sunshine. Hank met Claire's eyes and grinned. "Any requests?"

"Surprise me," Claire said, grinning back. "I like your surprises."

"Wise girl." Hank shuffled through the records. "Hey, look at that, a record called 'Graveyard Dream Blues!'"

"No blues," Claire pleaded.

"Ah, here we go." Hank chose a record, and placed it over the spindle. "If there's any level ground, go stand on it and get ready to dance while I give this thing a crank."

Smiling with pure delight, Claire stood up and watched him wind the handle. The familiar hissing and crackling came out of the bell as he put the needle down.

"May I?" Hank bowed from the waist with one arm outstretched and then in one smooth sweep stood up and took Claire in his arms.

The music began, a Bessie Smith song about love and good times. They danced among the gravestones in the sun, with the breeze on their cheeks and the birds watching from the trees.

"Oops, pardon me, sir," Hank said as he bumped into a gravestone.

"That's old Mr. Ledue," Claire said, letting him spin her around. "I doubt he'd mind. Whooa! The grass is so slippery."

"Don't fall in with him! Think he'd get up and dance if he thought he could cut in?"

Claire tipped her head back and laughed. "I expect he would."

"A man after my own heart."

"I know something about your heart, too," Claire said, grinning mischievously at him. "I know your taste in novels, Logan."

He arched his eyebrows. "Oh?"

"*Tess of the D'Urbervilles?* Really, Hank, you'll never convince me you're so tough if you read books like that."

"What a little snoop you are," he murmured, twining his fingers through hers and pulling her closer. "I like that."

She laughed, and they danced until the song ended and Hank bounded back to flip the record.

"Hang on!" he warned.

As Hank pulled her back into his arms, Claire felt a rush of such joy that she thought she could simply step off the crest of Burial Hill and dance across Marblehead's rooftops. There was no kidding herself any longer: she was heart and soul in love with Hank Logan, no matter who he was or what he might have done.

"Promise me you're not a murdering rumrunner," Claire murmured, looking up into his eyes.

He turned her around. The music was slowing, and the song ended. The needle skipped and bumped at the center of the record, whispering nothing into the air, but Claire and Hank continued to dance, their steps slower and slower until they stopped, their arms around one another. Then Hank kissed her, and Claire forgot everything.

"I love you," he whispered, moving his lips to her ear.

She closed her eyes. She felt faint and her pulse was racing. "Do you?" she breathed as he kissed her throat.

All Claire could think was how very sweet it was to let go, to let someone gather her up and carry her for a while. No wonder her mother was so hopeful, so willing to overlook Handy's flaws. Claire thought she herself could overlook anything that Hank said or did, as long as he said he loved her.

"Claire, tell me if you love me," Hank said. "Tell me, and I'll answer your question."

She sighed, and rested her cheek against his shoulder. "Yes. I love you."

"I didn't do it," he said, kissing her hair. "I didn't do it, you've got to believe me."

"I do believe you. I love you," she whispered. "I didn't want to, but I can't help it. I love you so much it hurts."

He tightened his arms around her. "Then what happened last night?"

"Last night?" Claire looked up at him, puzzled.

To her surprise, Hank was blushing. "Why did you say it was nothing, when I kissed you last night? It wasn't nothing to me."

Claire smiled and put her hand to his cheek. "Oh, what idiots we are. I'm sorry. I thought you didn't mean it, so—"

"So you pretended it didn't matter, and then I thought you didn't care so like a sap I agreed," Hank said, rolling his eyes. "And that clinched it for you. Aren't we a regular pair of beauties?"

With a laugh, Claire stepped out of Hank's arms. She felt breathless and had to steady herself against a gravestone. She kept her gaze on the wide, gray glittering ocean instead of on Hank, because if she looked at him, she wouldn't be able to speak.

"Then I'll try to tell you plain," she said quietly. "No tough talk, no boxing match. I've never felt this before but I know I'm crazy for you. We'll either find who killed Tink or we won't, but either way, you'll leave Marblehead and never come back, and I guess I'll never get over it. And if that makes me a sap, I can't help it." Her hands were trembling.

"Claire, don't—"

"That's the end of my pretty speech," Claire said brightly, turning around to smile at him. She drew a shaky breath. "And that's going to stay the end or I'll be useless for anything. I do have work to do, as much as I would like to dance all day."

Hank tugged on his ear as he gave her a skeptical look. "All right, if that's the way you want it. We won't discuss it anymore—right now. But remember, MacKenzie, you don't fool me for a minute."

Claire felt a catch in her throat. She loved him so much she could hardly breathe.

"What are you going to do today?" she asked.

He began packing up the Victrola. "I'm going to take another look at that house on the Neck."

"I think it could be Swenson's house," Claire said, holding out her hands for the speaker. "I'm sure he's tied up in this whole thing somehow."

"Could be," Hank agreed. "I saw him at the Ship last night and happened to mention that we had a mutual acquaintance, a guy in the rackets in Chicago. This fellow is pretty obscure, not a well-known wise guy."

Claire put her hand on Hank's arm. "Did Swenson say he knew him?"

"Nope."

"Did you really figure he would?" Claire asked. They began to pick their way down the hill in single file, Hank in the lead so he could help her down the steep parts.

"Why should he admit it to you? You could be a G-man for all he knows."

"Ha, me a cop! My pal Joe Tucci would get a laugh out of that one," Hank said wryly. "It was a shot in the dark, that's all."

A chill ran up Claire's neck. "Bad choice of words."

"So knock on wood," Hank said, rapping his head with his knuckles.

"Did you try something like that the other night when I saw you with him outside the Ship?"

Hank bit his lip. "Well . . . I might have dropped a few hints that maybe I could help him out, being a reporter and all. You know, write the true facts about how all this bootlegging and gangster stuff is just exaggerated. I thought he might go for it."

Claire shook her head in dismay. "Why didn't you tell me that before? You're still trying to protect me, aren't you?"

"Can't a guy be chivalrous around here?" he asked lightly, turning back to the path.

"Hank, maybe you shouldn't go."

He stopped to look back at her. Because the hill was so steep, he was below her. Hank took her hand and brought it to his lips.

"I'll be careful," he said, turning her hand over and kissing her palm.

Claire wanted to take him by the arms and not let go. But she didn't.

"Here, put that speaker on top. I'll take it the rest of

146

the way," Hank said. "You've got to put your toys back where you find them."

He turned to go.

"Promise me you'll come back," Claire said hoarsely.

"I'll meet you at the Rose for dinner, you can count on that. But say," he added, almost as an afterthought. "If I do happen to be late, why not give Joey a call? Federal Building, Boston."

Claire stared at him.

"Joseph Tucci," Hank said slowly, meeting her eyes. Then he gave her a confident smile, and walked away, the Victrola balanced on his hip.

Chapter Eleven

CLAIRE MADE HER way slowly back to the Wild Rose, shivering as she walked through the streets. She dreaded going home to the long, creeping hours of the afternoon, and to her mother.

When she opened the front door, there was an argument in progress in the foyer. Claire stepped inside to see the coal man, red-faced with bluster, waving a slip of paper at Mrs. MacKenzie.

"Three months overdue on this coal, Missus, I'm that surprised!" Mr. O'Hara said in his broad brogue. "I never thought it of you."

"Oh, but I tell you I don't remember signing a bill," Mrs. MacKenzie said. "And I don't remember taking any coal in June, surely I didn't sign it?"

"Right here is your signature, Missus," O'Hara declared, jabbing a grimy finger at the bill.

Claire took the bill from him, and glanced at the date. "Mother that was the day we had that party of boys up from Harvard, all asking for sandwiches and ice cream."

"Oh, I remember them," her mother said, brightening. "They were such gentlemen, but they were all over the place! I could hardly get my breath."

O'Hara screwed up his face. "Fine, and so you remember signing the bill now, Missus?"

"I'll pay you, Mr. O'Hara," Claire said calmly, passing him and going to the reception desk. She opened the checkbook and uncapped a pen. "I'm sorry for the misunderstanding."

The coal man shifted his feet. "Well, then, that's fine, and no hard feelings I'm sure, ladies."

When he was paid and gone, Mrs. MacKenzie put one hand to her flushed face. "Oh, I know I'm a ninny, but there he was carrying on in that unpleasant way of his —the Irish are so coarse, I always think."

"Forget it, don't fuss, Mother," Claire said, putting her forehead down on her hand. Claire closed her eyes as Mrs. MacKenzie continued explaining why she'd been so flustered, and how O'Hara had bullied her and put her in such a state—

"Mother, please," Claire said.

To Claire's dismay, Mrs. MacKenzie suddenly began to cry. While Claire sat frozen behind the desk, her mother groped her way to a chair and sat down, burying her face in a handkerchief. After a moment, Claire roused herself and went to Mrs. MacKenzie's side.

"Did he upset you that much?" Claire asked, patting her mother's shoulder.

"It's not that," her mother said, waving her handkerchief in a forlorn gesture. "Oh, I don't know what to do, I wasn't cut out for this work. When your father was alive I felt I could manage, but ever since he died I feel so helpless all the time and I know you think I'm pathetic."

Claire gulped. "No, Mother. No."

"Oh, you do, I know you do," Mrs. MacKenzie wailed. "And now you think Jack Handy is a good-for-nothing crook and what if you're right about that, too?" She sobbed into her handkerchief.

"Maybe I'm not," Claire said without conviction. She looked down at her mother's bent head and felt pity creeping up and tugging on her like a crying baby.

The door opened, and a young couple walked into the inn. With another sob, Mrs. MacKenzie flung herself out of her chair and ran out of the room.

"Oh, excuse us," the man said uncertainly, backing up to the door.

Claire took a deep breath. "Please come in. How can I help you?"

"We were hoping to get a room for a couple of nights?"

"Of course." Claire opened the register and placed a pen in the crease of the book, each movement slow and precise. She didn't know how she could get through the day until Hank returned.

"We've heard so much about this town," the young woman said with an adoring look at her husband. "We heard it was very romantic."

150

"Any town is romantic with you in it, Sweetie-pie," he said, touching her nose with one finger.

The woman giggled. "Bert!"

Claire looked down at the register. "Dinner is at six o'clock, Mr. and Mrs. Higgins."

"That's great," Mr. Higgins said. He gave his wife a wink and then leaned toward Claire and lowered his voice. "Any place in this town where you can—you know . . . ?" He made a quick tippling motion with one hand.

"I'm sorry, I don't know what you mean," Claire said, meeting his eyes without blinking.

"Never mind, Bert," Mrs. Higgins said, her pretty face pink with embarrassment. She plucked at his sleeve.

But he was not so easily defeated. "You know," he repeated coaxingly. "Where you can get a drink—*you* know."

Claire gave the man an amused look. "You might try asking our chief of police," she said wryly.

Mr. Higgins gaped at her. "Hey, I was—I was just joking, sister, I don't mean anything by it. Forget it."

"Oh, Bert," the wife said. She bit her lip.

"Mr. and Mrs. Higgins, let me show you to your room," Claire said, trying not to smile.

The rest of the afternoon dragged on with chores and errands and accounts. Claire found herself glancing at each clock she passed and at the sky through every window. Already it seemed that Hank had been gone far too long; it shouldn't take all afternoon to snoop around one house. The waiting was exhausting, and once Claire even picked up the telephone, determined to call Boston.

But if he was waiting and watching the house for the people in it to leave, there was no telling how long it might be, she told herself with an attempt at common sense. Hank might be ambitious and bold, but he would hardly walk into an occupied house and start looking around for evidence of smuggling. Claire tried to picture him brashly bluffing his way out of a confrontation with six gangsters brandishing tommy guns and managed a faint laugh.

"He could probably do it, too," she muttered as she began setting the tables for dinner.

Her hand rested on the back of the old Windsor chair where he'd sat on his first night at the inn. Frowning, she traced one finger along the edge and down to the arm as though she could sense him there.

Suddenly, the waiting was unbearable. She had to have someone to talk to, she had to feel she was doing something. Claire knew it was foolish, but if she left the house she thought perhaps Hank would return in her absence—like taking an umbrella on a picnic to be certain it wouldn't rain.

She left the last of the napkins in a pile on the sideboard and let herself out of the house. The wind was picking up, shooing bits of scrap paper ahead of Claire down the street. She hurried around the corner and down a twisting alley. Around another corner was the narrow, rickety old house where Tink Trelawney had lived. Claire knocked on the door.

"Hello, Claire," Kitty said when she opened it. She sounded tired.

Claire could see past Kitty into the small front room, where there were open boxes and crates. Claire looked swiftly at her friend. "Are you packing up?"

"I'm leaving." Kitty glanced up at the doorway of her house and shrugged. "I'll try my chances in Boston."

"But don't you want to wait until the man who killed your father is caught?" Claire asked.

"What difference would that make? My dad will still be dead."

Claire shook her head. "Doesn't justice matter?"

"Justice? Don't make me laugh, Claire," Kitty said. "If there was any justice there'd be a lot more people shot than my poor old dad who never hurt anyone but himself." She stood rigid in the doorway, the narrow, bent, dour old house looming up behind her like narrow, bent, dour old Tink himself.

Claire almost shuddered. "Come out with me," she said, taking her friend's hand. "Come for a walk with me, away from here."

"All right," Kitty said tonelessly. She pulled Tink's old oilskin off a hook and shut the door behind her without a backward glance. They linked arms and walked up the street in silence.

Claire couldn't think of any words that wouldn't sound trivial in the face of Kitty's mourning, and yet she knew there was a reason to find Tink's murderer. It wouldn't bring Tink back. But it mattered.

The two girls walked past the harbor and up to the

park, where they sat side by side on a bench, the sun sinking behind them and the wind fresh on their faces. Below them, in the harbor, Tink's grubby old fishing boat was still docked.

"Kitty, it may not seem important now, but I think it will, later," Claire said gently. "Has Chief Handy said anything to you about the investigation?"

Kitty shrugged one shoulder, not even looking at Claire. She dug her hands deep into the pockets of her father's raincoat.

"Has he asked you any questions about what Tink had been doing lately?" Claire probed. "Has he asked to look around the house? Anything?"

"Not to speak of," Kitty said. She frowned and turned to Claire with a visible effort at concentration. "He doesn't seem to be trying too hard."

Claire tucked her hair behind her ear as the wind swirled it across her eyes. She thought she knew why he wasn't trying very hard.

"What had Tink been up to, lately?" she asked, watching Kitty closely. "Did he ever say anything to you that seemed odd, did he act different before he died?"

"Well . . ." Kitty chewed on a fingernail. "He did seem a bit different, I guess, a bit pleased with himself. Cat that swallowed the canary, like that. Sort of smug."

Claire felt a thrill of satisfaction: she was sure she had been right about Tink. "How long had he been like that?" she pressed.

"For a few weeks, maybe," Kitty said with another shrug. "I can't really remember. But he was boasting one

154

night that folks around here were going to get a different opinion of him, and wouldn't they be surprised. That some people would have to sit up and take notice of Tink Trelawney at last."

"What did he mean?" Claire asked, her eyes wide.

"Just boasting," Kitty said. "I didn't take him seriously. He got grand notions all the time."

"I think it was different this time." Claire glanced down at the harbor at the *Kittiwake*.

Beside her, Kitty sighed. She was looking down at her father's boat, too. "Maybe. If he had any good luck coming to him, it'd be typical: just when things start going right, along comes something wrong."

Claire hugged her arms around herself, shivering in the breeze. "Kitty," she said gently. "I think he was working for bootleggers."

"Ah, Pop," Kitty whispered, still looking at Tink's boat. Her throat worked hard as she swallowed.

Claire had to look away. "I think he must have tried to turn the tables on his boss."

"Or opened his big mouth in the wrong company," Kitty said sadly. She roused herself, and put one hand over Claire's. "I think I want to go home."

"Come eat dinner with us at the Rose," Claire urged.

"No, I'd rather not. But thanks all the same."

Claire shivered again as she stood up and gave her friend a sympathetic look.

"Here, take this," Kitty said, shrugging out of the coat. "I'm not cold."

"No, you don't have to do that," Claire said. "I'm fine."

"Go on, I've got a sweater," Kitty said. She put the macintosh around Claire's shoulders.

Claire pulled it close, grateful for the warmth and for Kitty's kind heart. "Thanks."

The girls left their bench and parted ways at the entrance of the park. Claire walked home slowly, not daring to get her hopes up that Hank might have returned. She stopped outside the front door, almost afraid to open it. But she made herself go in. Bob was sitting at the desk, sighing heavily over a schoolbook. He darted Claire a wary look as she entered.

"Has Mr. Logan come in?" Claire asked.

Bob turned a page. "Nope."

She paced the foyer, head down, aware of the distant murmur of voices from the dining room. Her mother would need her to work, but Claire couldn't go in. Hank had promised to be back by dinnertime. She put her hands into the pockets of Trelawney's coat, frowning.

"Claire?"

Glancing up, Claire saw that Bob was watching her with anxious eyes. She wondered if he saw how fearful she was for Hank's sake, and her heart went out to her brother in gratitude.

"I'm going to stop drinking," he said. "Honest."

Claire felt a mixture of relief and irritation. With an effort, she wrenched her thoughts away from Hank. "What about Hope?" she asked.

"Will you talk to her?" he asked. He jumped from his

chair, his face bright and eager. "Say you will, I know she'll listen to you."

For a moment, Claire drove her fists deep into her pockets and bowed her head. She felt as if she were flying in a hundred pieces. "Yes," she whispered tightly. "I'll do it."

"Oh, you're the best, Claire," Bob exulted, running to the door. "I'll go get her."

Claire stared sightlessly at the carpet, trying to gather herself and put things into their proper order. Gradually, she became aware that she was folding and unfolding a bit of paper with her fingers. She pulled it out of the pocket and looked at it.

There was a phone number written on it and the name Garrison. Claire glanced at the telephone on the desk, then took the receiver off the hook and read the number to the operator.

"Yeah?" came a low voice when the line was answered.

Claire wasn't sure what she was doing. "Garrison?" she asked.

"Yeah."

A distant burst of laughter came from the dining room. Claire took a blind leap. "I need to speak to Swenson."

There was a weighty silence on the line. Then the man spoke again. "Who's asking?"

"I—" Claire cleared her throat. "I wanted—" She fought desperately to think of something to say.

The line was cut off. Claire stood staring at the telephone for a long moment. "Hank," she breathed. "I've got to help you."

She turned and hurried out of the Wild Rose, not sure at all what she was going to do. She felt helpless with frustration and uncertainty, and yearned to get nearer to Hank. The thought of him out on the Neck, just across the harbor, drew her to the waterfront. As she rounded the corner of a building she caught sight of a figure on the *Kittiwake,* and for one horrifying, superstitious moment, thought it was Trelawney.

Then she recognized Chief Handy. Claire watched him cast off the bow and stern lines, and retreat back into the pilothouse. The engine started with a faint grumble. Water churned whitely at the stern as the boat moved away from the dock.

"What are you doing?" Claire whispered.

With growing uneasiness, she ran down the street to Kitty's house again and knocked loudly. She spoke the moment her friend opened the door. "I just saw Chief Handy take your father's boat out."

Kitty shrugged. "He offered to sell it for me. He said he's got a buyer in Salem, and I should get enough money to make a start in Boston."

"He's taking the *Kittiwake* to Salem?" Claire asked in a doubtful voice.

"To sell it," Kitty repeated. "Are you all right, Claire?"

Claire focused her eyes on Kitty's face. "I'm not sure." She turned away, more confused and worried than ever.

Down the street, light spilled from the windows of

Curly's Drug Store. Claire went in, the bell tinkling over the door as she shut it behind her.

"Evening, Claire," Mr. Curly called.

A few shoppers looked Claire's way. She nodded hello to them and slipped into the telephone booth, fishing a nickel out of her pocket. The coin fell with a jingle into the telephone and Claire eased herself down on the seat to wait for an operator.

"What number, please?"

"Can you connect me with the Federal Building in Boston?" Claire asked, darting a nervous look through the glass door.

"What's that? You'll have to speak louder, dear," the operator complained.

Claire turned her back to the store. Until she saw Hank safe again, she trusted no one in Marblehead. "Federal Building in Boston," she repeated as loudly as she dared.

"That's a toll call."

"I know, I know," Claire whispered, dragging out all the change in her pockets. "Please make the connection."

With a sniff, the operator told her how much money to drop into the phone, and a few moments later, Claire heard the distant ringing.

"Can I speak with Joseph Tucci?" Claire asked as soon as she was through.

"What depahtment?" It was a strong Boston accent.

"Oh—he's—" Claire looked out into the drug store again. To her eyes, it seemed everyone was trying to listen.

Mr. Curly was wiping down the soda fountain counter with a blue checkered towel.

"What depahtment?" the Boston operator asked again.

"FBI," Claire said. "That's all I know. He's—"

"I'll connect you now."

For several moments, Claire heard nothing but the faint, crackling hiss of the telephone wires vibrating between Marblehead and Boston. Then a voice, surprisingly close, spoke in her ear.

"Tucci."

"Mr. Tucci, my name is Claire MacKenzie. I live—"

"In Marblehead," he cut in. "Sure, I've heard all about *you*."

The color rushed to Claire's face. "Mr. Tucci, this afternoon Hank went out to a house which I believe is owned by a man named Swenson. Does that mean anything to you? Or the name Garrison?"

There was a pause. Claire counted heartbeats in her head. The bell over the drug store door tinkled loudly.

"How long has he been gone?"

Claire swallowed. "Since lunchtime," she said, her eyes scanning the store nervously. "Mr. Tucci, do you know who Swenson is?"

"Yes, Miss MacKenzie, I do. We know he's in the rum rackets, but we've never been able to get anything on him. He's more slippery than Capone. He's the mastermind, never gets anywhere near the illegal stuff."

Claire closed her eyes. Hank was out there on his

own. Bold, foolhardy Hank Logan, hot after a story, afraid of nothing.

"Miss MacKenzie?" Tucci's voice was urgent. "Are you still there?"

"I'm here, Mr. Tucci," Claire whispered. "But I'm going to hang up now. I'm going to look for Hank."

"Stay where you are, please! We'll leave right now."

"But you're over an hour away," Claire said, her voice so steady she was surprised. "You might be too late."

"Miss MacKenzie. Claire! Stay put!"

She hung up the telephone. "Like hell I will."

Chapter Twelve

CLAIRE STEPPED OUT onto the sidewalk, her mind racing. There was no time to wonder if she was doing the right thing. She made for the Little Harbor, her shadow running with her. Hank was out at Swenson's, and she didn't believe for a moment that Handy was taking the *Kittiwake* to Salem. She had a hunch that Handy was on his way out around the Neck with Tink's boat, and Claire didn't like it one bit. There was no way on earth she could sit idly by, waiting for Tucci. She had to go out there and see for herself.

A dog barked somewhere as she hurried to Zeke Penworthy's dinghy, her footsteps thudding loudly on the dock. Claire stepped down onto the seat, and the boat rocked beneath her. With her eyes on the mouth of the harbor, she reached under the bow for the key. It fell into her hand and she put it in the ignition and pulled the cord at the same time. The engine caught, and in a moment she had cast off and was steering the small craft out into open water in the fading light.

As she came out of sheltered Little Harbor into the main waterway, the tide and the wind both tugged at the boat. Claire clutched the tiller with one hand and pulled Tink's oilskin tight around her shoulders with the other. She strained to see ahead.

There was no sign of the *Kittiwake* or any boat to the north, toward Salem. There was only the rolling gray water, the gray sky, the bleak rocky coastline. Handy was not taking the *Kittiwake* that way.

Claire shook her hair back out of her eyes. The wind was strong, and toward the east where the open ocean lay, whitecaps curled; a fine spray blew against Claire's face, cold and damp. She brushed a wet curl from her cheek and made for the out-thrust fist of rock at the end of the Neck, the sound of the little motor swallowed up by the surrounding sky. Spray tore off the bow into the wind as the hull bounced against oncoming waves with sharp slaps.

And once Claire rounded the shelter of the Neck, the elements were even stronger. The surf foamed and groaned around the granite boulders that spilled off the end of Marblehead Neck, sucking back in great gulps and surging up again. Claire ignored the threat of the rocks and kept her course, her cheeks stinging with cold and salt.

She had to find Hank. That was all she could think about. She scanned the land, where the big summer houses were silhouetted against the western sky. They were dark and silent, their windows shuttered against the oncoming winter. A more lonesome and desolate sight could not exist, Claire thought, than empty houses facing the great gray ocean.

But they were not all empty. Hank was in one of them.

Claire guessed she was near Swenson's. She made for a dock hidden from the rest of the coastline by an outcropping of rock where the surf boomed and flung up streamers of white. The wind filled her ears when she cut the motor. Claire grabbed for a piling, making fast the bowline. Her hands were icy.

With just a glance up at the deserted house, Claire clambered out of the boat and ran off the dock. Wild rose bushes grew between boulders, whipped bare by the wind. She shouldered her way through, her heart pounding, praying that she had guessed right and that Swenson's was just ahead. Stumbling, Claire scraped her hand on a rock and then looked cautiously around a boulder. Before her was a view of Swenson's dock.

The *Kittiwake* was tied fast beside the powerboat.

For her mother's sake, Claire still hoped that her suspicions were wrong, that Handy was investigating Tink's murder and had tracked down Swenson just as Claire and Hank had.

But somehow she didn't think so.

She huddled in the shelter of the rocks, blowing on her hands, and tried to think what to do. The wind moaned fitfully over a crack in the granite, grating at Claire's nerves.

The *Kittiwake* was grinding and scraping against the dock. Claire could hear the hull bumping wood each time there was a lull in the wind. That was no way to dock a boat, Claire knew, and wondered why Handy would be so careless with it. She counted heartbeats while she scanned the area between dock and house. There were no signs of life. The light was failing quickly.

Claire groaned and put her forehead down on her knee. "Think," she whispered. "Do something. Is he here or isn't he?"

She stared at the ground, willing herself to action. After a moment, she realized she was looking at a cigarette butt, the brand that Hank smoked. Her stomach churned. She saw her hand tremble as she picked it up and crumbled it between her fingers: the tobacco was fresh, the paper clean and white.

"Hank," Claire breathed. "Where *are* you?"

She took a deep breath and looked up at the house again, and the door to the terrace opened. A man backed out, clumsily bearing something before him. As he emerged, Chief Handy followed: between them, they carried a man's body.

The wind filled Claire's ears. As Handy and the other man carried their burden down to the dock, Claire strained to see. Handy stopped and shifted his grip, and Claire saw Hank's face as his head lolled to the side.

"Damn you, Hank," she gasped. "Don't be dead. Please don't be dead."

Her eyes burned as she stared in the face of the wind. Handy and his partner—the man with binoculars, Claire

saw—carried Hank roughly on board the *Kittiwake* and
into the pilothouse, and jumped back down onto the
dock. Handy stood looking out to sea, shoulders hunched
against the wind, while the other man walked away.

"Garrison!" Handy turned to shout into the wind.

The man stopped and looked back, and Handy
pointed at his wristwatch. Garrison nodded and contin
ued to the house.

Claire watched Handy, and her heart filled with such
outrage that she thought she could push him into the
ocean with the force of her hatred.

If Claire had had a gun, she would gladly have used
it.

Handy watched as Garrison came back with two gas
oline cans. Claire tasted bile in her throat as they boarded
the *Kittiwake* with the cans. She couldn't let herself imag
ine what they were doing, she just knew she had to get to
Hank. In a moment, the old boat's engine started and
Garrison jumped off. The *Kittiwake,* bow pointing to the
open ocean, slowly moved away from the dock, and
Handy hurried out of the pilothouse and jumped off.

Helpless and shaking, Claire watched the two men
on the dock. The *Kittiwake* lumbered slowly out against
the oncoming waves, and after a minute or so, Handy and
Garrison walked back toward the house.

In an instant, Claire scrambled out of her hiding
place and tore back toward the motorboat. Thorns
dragged at her as she forced her way through the bushes,
and she plunged, gasping, down the slope to the little
dock where her boat waited. She started the engine, throt-

tled it high and pointed the bow for open water. Its hull smacked against the waves as it raced forward.

Rounding the promontory, Claire saw the unpiloted *Kittiwake* ahead of her on the water. It made little headway against the running current that dragged it southward, rolling heavily in the swells. In such hard wind and heavy seas, the boat would be forced to run aground, and if Hank wasn't already dead, he'd surely drown. Claire didn't waste a look back toward Swenson's, but scanned the dark coastline. It was all rock and pounding surf.

She throttled the motor as high as it would go. The little boat bucked wildly on the waves and spray lashed at her in stinging gusts, but she was gaining on the *Kittiwake* and Hank. Now she could hear the low rumble of the fishing boat's engine.

Breathing hard, she coiled a line with one hand, her eyes on the *Kittiwake*. The gap between the two boats narrowed dangerously, and Claire let go the tiller, stood up and threw the line over the *Kittiwake*'s side. The rope snaked away whitely in the dim light, landed, and then slithered back, falling into the water. Claire hauled it out, her hands wet and cold. Again she threw it, sobbing with the effort of whipping it around a cleat. The dinghy bumped against the larger boat, upsetting Claire's balance, but the rope caught and Claire grabbed the end.

"Hank!" she shouted. The wind tore her voice from her throat. *"Hank!"*

There was no answer. Claire made her boat fast to the *Kittiwake* and idled the engine. Both boats heaved up and down on the waves, and a quick look told Claire they were being pushed steadily toward the rocks. She closed her eyes, almost faint with fear and then lunged upward, grabbing at the gunwale. A wave sent the *Kittiwake* rolling up as her boat pitched down and for a horrifying moment, her feet swung free and all her weight dragged on her cold hands. Then she kicked hard and hauled herself up. She fell over the side and collapsed on the deck in a pool of gasoline.

"My God!" Claire struggled frantically to her feet. The deck was awash in gasoline, the fumes stinging her eyes. The slightest spark would blow the boat sky-high.

"Hank!"

She ran into the pilothouse. Hank was lying slumped against the bulkhead just where Trelawney had lain. With a sob, Claire ran to him and put her hand on his throat. His pulse beat beneath her fingers.

"Hank!"

He groaned, and Claire grabbed the lapels of his jacket in both fists, hanging her head in relief. Then she shook him. "Wake up! Hank, wake up!"

Desperate, she stood up. At least she could steer the boat away from the rocks. But the wheel was gone. Handy must have ripped it out: there was no way to control the boat. Claire gulped down her fear and went back to Hank.

"I have to get you out of here," she said in a shaking voice. She grabbed his arms and dragged him backward out of the pilothouse into the open air. Off the starboard bow, the coast loomed dark.

Hank was a dead weight in her arms as she propped him up against the gunwale.

"Hank, wake up! *Please! Help me!*"

She gasped with the effort, struggling to get him up. Almost sobbing, she heaved him up onto the gunwale and turned him around until he hung limp with his legs dangling overboard and his arms and torso inside. Claire leaned out and squinted down into the darkness. The smaller motorboat, six feet down, rose up and down with the *Kittiwake.* Waves pounded on the rocks, only yards away, and gasoline washed over her shoes.

"I'm sorry, Hank," Claire said. She grabbed his wrists and shoved at him until he began to slip backward. Panting, she hung overboard and stared into his face. Then she let go and he fell in a heap in the dinghy.

Her hands shook as she dragged the line from around the cleat and swung herself over. She hung off the side of the *Kittiwake,* her feet kicking out for the other boat. A wave bounced the little boat up and she fell into it beside Hank.

The sound of waves crashing against the rocks was deafening as Claire throttled the motor up again and pulled away from the old fishing boat. They sliced over the waves into open water, the wind fierce and cold in Claire's face. Behind her, she heard a splintering thud as the *Kittiwake* struck rock. She looked back, and the old boat listed hard as a wave drove it against the rocks again. The engine rumbled, another wave crashed at it again, and suddenly the boat exploded with a deafening roar.

Claire ducked and a wave of heat immediately hit her back. She fell forward over Hank's body, but didn't let go of the tiller. The little boat sped forward through the orange glare of fire, the spray from the bow glittering like diamonds against the purple sky.

Claire couldn't see Hank's face but she heard him groan. "Don't leave me now," she whispered. "Don't you dare leave me now."

The light was fading fast. She steered the boat up along the Neck, frantic to reach the harbor and a doctor. But when she neared Swenson's she changed her mind, as the place was ablaze with lights, and a Coast Guard cutter was tied up at the dock. A crowd milled about on the lawn, and as she pulled the boat into the shadow of the cutter, she saw that most of the men were in uniform. Swenson, Handy, and Garrison were in the center. Claire stayed hidden, trying to decide what to do.

"I don't know what you're talking about!" Handy was yelling at a short, dark-haired man in a trench coat. "That guy Logan was trespassing, so naturally Mr. Swenson called the police."

"Where did he go?"

"Listen, Agent Tucci, how should I know? He left here under his own steam."

There was a stir at the back of the crowd and Mrs. MacKenzie and Bob pushed to the front. "Where's Claire?" Mrs. MacKenzie cried, grabbing Handy by the arm. "That man thinks Claire is here somewhere!"

"Now, Ellie, just keep out of this," Handy shouted. "I haven't seen her."

"If you hurt my sister!" Bob said, his voice breaking.

"I haven't seen her," Handy retorted.

Nobody noticed Claire's boat in the shadows. She

was shivering uncontrollably from the cold, and could hardly tie a knot in the boat's mooring line. Her heart pounded.

"You're all trespassing," Swenson spoke up. "This is outrageous. Tucci, get your men out of here."

"Not until we find out what's going on. There was an explosion out on the water, we've had some serious accusations, and I'm just a little bit suspicious," Agent Tucci said in a firm voice. "So how about we just find out what the hell is going on here?"

"Where's Claire?" Mrs. MacKenzie asked again, her voice high with panic.

Handy rounded on her angrily. "Just keep out of this!" he yelled. "And you, Tucci! Get your men out of here, there's nothing to investigate."

"Yes, there is," Bob said, turning to Tucci. In the glare of the lights he looked pale and sick. "You can start with the speakeasy Handy runs at the Ship."

"Shut up!" Handy roared. "Shut up you stupid kid! You're nothing but a drunk."

"He runs it with Swenson," Bob said, raising his voice. "He told me all about it, told me we could do the same thing at the Wild Rose and make a bundle."

Handy lunged for Bob, but two uniformed officers held him back. "Shut up! Shut up!" he screamed wildly.

"Jack, no—" Mrs. MacKenzie held out one hand. Then she shook her head and looked at him in disbelief. "You bastard," she choked out.

"Where are Hank Logan and Claire MacKenzie?" Tucci asked.

Claire walked forward. Her head felt light, but she focused on her mother and brother. "I'm here," she said, her voice hoarse.

Everyone turned to stare at her and Mrs. MacKenzie let out a cry. "Claire!" She rushed forward and enveloped Claire in a fierce hug.

"I'm all right, Mother," Claire said, pressing her face against her mother's shoulder. "I'm all right."

Someone touched her arm. "Where's Logan?" Tucci asked in a low, urgent voice.

Claire drew herself up and pointed at Chief Handy and Garrison. "They put him on a boat and rigged it to explode. They tried to murder Hank," she said levelly. "I saw them. I can make a full statement."

"That's a goddamn lie!" Handy shouted, struggling against his captors. "She set me up, she's always been against me!"

Tucci stepped toward Claire. "Where's Hank now?"

"In that motorboat," Claire said. Her knees buckled and Tucci caught her as she fell. "He's in the boat," she whispered as she fainted.

She woke up on a leather couch in an elegant living room, her head on someone's lap.

"The least excitement and she passes out," a familiar voice said above her.

Claire opened her eyes. Hank was smiling down at her, holding an icebag to his head.

"I saved your life, you bum," she said. She sat up

172

unsteadily. Someone had put a coat around her and she pulled it tight, shivering a little.

They looked at one another silently. Claire was too filled with emotion to speak and was afraid she would begin to cry with joy and relief. The windows rattled in the wind and Claire broke away from Hank's steady gaze.

"Where are we?" she asked, shivering again.

"Swenson's living room," Hank said with a glance around. "Pretty ritzy, isn't it? Of course, I wouldn't have chosen this color for the wallpaper."

"Hank, I—" Claire began.

"Hey, she's awake," Tucci said, coming into the living room with two steaming mugs.

"Joe, let me introduce Claire MacKenzie," Hank said with his old cocky grin.

Tucci handed Claire a mug of coffee. "I've met Miss MacKenzie already, Logan." He smiled at Claire and she returned his smile gratefully.

"What happened to Handy and Swenson?" Claire asked, cupping her hands around the hot mug.

"They're still trying to explain the cases of rum Hank found in the basement," Tucci said. "Between Bob's statement and yours, they're in a pretty deep hole, and that snake Garrison is already singing like a bird."

"Why did they kill Tink?" Claire asked. "It *was* them, wasn't it?"

Tucci rubbed his face tiredly. There were circles under his dark eyes. "According to Garrison, Trelawney did pickups for them long enough to figure out that Chief Handy never sold the Ship at all and was running the speakeasy. So he was trying a little blackmail. It was Handy who shot him."

"Oh, God. Please don't tell my mother," Claire pleaded.

"There's no way to keep it from her," Hank said, putting his hand on Claire's shoulder. "You can't save everyone."

"She sure saved you, though," Tucci said to Hank. He smiled at Claire. "I had a feeling she would."

Claire shook her head. "Why do you say that? You don't even know me."

"I know enough. I heard plenty about you from Logan."

"Shut up," Hank growled.

"Oh, sure," Tucci continued. "You should've heard him go on about you. How he came to sleepy old Marblehead looking for heroes and drama from the past, and found the bravest, most beautiful—"

Hank threw the icebag at his friend. Tucci caught it and stood up. Claire ducked her head over her coffee mug, smiling blissfully.

"Don't you have some official business to attend to, Agent Tucci?" Hank asked. "Suspects to beat up or something?"

Tucci looked from Hank to Claire and shrugged. His eyes twinkled. "Maybe I do at that. Oh, by the way, Claire, your mother and brother and his friend Hope Carter are in the next room. Should I . . . ?"

"In a minute," Hank said, looking at Claire.

Claire and Hank didn't speak as Tucci left the room.

When the door shut, Claire felt suddenly shy and awkward. She blew on her coffee.

"I guess you got your scoop," she said.

"Actually, there's a crowd of reporters here already," Hank said with a grimace. "The vultures."

Claire was almost afraid to look at him. "So now what?" she asked, trying to keep her voice light.

Instead of answering, Hank reached for her coffee mug and put it on the floor. Then he took both her hands. "I still have that book to write," he said. "I'm thinking about finding a nice homey little place, a respectable old inn—there's one here in town, in fact. It's called the Wild Rose. Ever hear of it?"

"How long will it take you to write the book?" Claire whispered.

"Quite a while, probably until they repeal this stupid Prohibition," Hank said. "After all, you've got to have champagne at a wedding."

Claire grinned. "You're pretty sure of yourself, aren't you, Logan?"

"Pretty sure, Clair-de-lune."

Claire threw her arms around his neck. "Me, too."

Follow the sweeping saga of generations
of young MacKenzie women, all growing up
at the Wild Rose Inn.

GRACE OF THE WILD ROSE INN
1944

*Grace MacKenzie has been achingly lonely since her
brother, Mark, and her fiancé, Jimmy Penworthy, left
to fight the war in Europe. While she waits for their
return, Grace finds independence and inner strength,
managing her family's Wild Rose Inn.*

*When the boys finally come home, Grace is heartbroken
at how the war has changed Jimmy. He brags about his
wartime heroics while stubbornly insisting that Grace
give up her dream of running the inn after they marry.
Grace is angry and confused—yet she also feels guilty
that she's not the girl Jimmy remembers and wants her
to be.*

*But Jimmy's army buddy Mike, who has come to Mar-
blehead, is everything Grace hoped to find in Jimmy.
Can Grace follow the path of her heart without sacrific-
ing her future or hurting those who love her?*

BRIDIE OF THE WILD ROSE INN
1695

Sixteen-year-old Bridie MacKenzie has waited ten years in Scotland to join her parents in the Massachusetts Bay Colony. Bridie's happiness at being reunited with her family is tempered by the reality of her new life. Her loving parents work day and night to make ends meet at their small, rough inn, and they have had to give up their religion for Puritanism under the colony's law.

Spirited Bridie refuses to conform to the rules—she vows not to give up either her faith or the healing herbs she has brought from Scotland. But all that Bridie believes in, the Puritans denounce as witchcraft. The price of holding on to her convictions may be high. Must Bridie lose her new home, her reputation, and her first true love for what she believes?

ANN OF THE WILD ROSE INN
1774

The dangers are terrifying for Ann MacKenzie and her twin brother, John, but both of them are willing to involve themselves in smuggling and other risky activities—anything to help their struggling country.

Marblehead, home to the Wild Rose Inn that's been in Ann's family since they first came to America nearly one hundred years ago, is no longer the tranquil place it once was. Tensions have increased between England and the colonies, and the locals resent the presence of the British military.

Ann does, too, until she falls in love with a handsome, sensitive young man she meets along the shore—a stranger who turns out to be a British sailor. Loving the enemy is wrong, but Ann can't help herself. Where should her allegiance lie? With her family and country, or with the love of her life?

EMILY OF THE WILD ROSE INN
1858

Emily MacKenzie is content spending her days sailing and working at the Wild Rose Inn with Lucy, her best friend and adopted sister. The rift between the North and South is growing, but Emily has never given much thought to the troubling social issues of the day, nor to the dangerous work of the Underground Railroad in her own town.

But conflict ensnares Emily when the Stockwells, a wealthy southern family, come to stay at the Inn with their slave, Moses. Emily knows in her heart that slavery is wrong, and wishes she could help Moses. But her growing feelings for Blount, the Stockwells' son, hold her back. By helping Moses, she would betray Blount, but taking Blount's side would compromise her values and destroy her heartfelt friendship with Lucy, a free black. Can Emily find the strength to do what must be done?

LAURA OF THE WILD ROSE INN
1898

On the eve of the twentieth century, the world is changing rapidly, and sixteen-year-old Laura MacKenzie wants to be a part of the coming age. Her parents, forever entrenched in their old-fashioned ways, are running the Wild Rose Inn the same way their family has for two centuries. Laura is sure there must be more to life than she finds in rustic Marblehead, Massachusetts, if only she were given the chance to leave and seek her destiny for herself.

When Laura meets Grant Van Doren, a student at Yale, she's introduced to new possibilities. Laura can almost taste the freedom and adventures Grant and the new era offer her. Under Grant's spell, all seems possible. Can Laura depend on Grant and his promises, or is her future something she must find for herself?

ABOUT THE AUTHOR

Jennifer Armstrong is the author of many books for children and young adults, including the historical novel *Steal Away*, the Pets, Inc., series, and several picture books.

Jennifer Armstrong lives in Saratoga Springs, New York, in a house more than 150 years old that is reputed to have been a tavern. In addition to writing, she raises guide-dog puppies and works in her garden, where roses grow around the garden gate.